ONE TO HOLD

By Tia Louise

Cover design by Regina Wamba of
MaeIDesign.com
Stock: **Thinkstock.com**

For the real-life hero who inspired this story.

Contents

CHAPTER 1 — A ONE-WEEK STAND

In the cool darkness of the semi-crowded bar, I could allow the last year to dissolve into a hazy fog, a far-off memory. Each low thump of bass that disappeared into the dull roar of voices beat it further down. With a little more alcohol, it could even become a dream — something that never occurred in real life. Something that could be brushed aside like a phantom, not a true form. Not a reality that burned shame, low and deep in my stomach.

Bars had become a thing of my past, along with flirtatious passes from unfamiliar men, but sitting alone in this hotel club, hundreds of miles from home, I felt wonderfully liberated. I could be anyone. Any anonymous woman having a drink before bed. I could pretend to be free.

My eyes traveled to the dance-floor where younger women in shiny slip dresses and chunky stilettos twisted and swayed, their smooth blonde or red hair matching their movements. They squeal-laughed when songs they liked came on, and the lines around their eyes disappeared as soon as their cheeks relaxed. They could dance all night and still make it to work tomorrow, eyes sparkling.

A bitter laugh slid from my throat as I stared back into the amber drink I'd ordered. The thought of dancing all night made me tired.

The bartender didn't notice me. I'd stood for almost five minutes trying to get his attention to order this drink, and it was gross. "Seven and seven" was all I could remember from the days when I used to order drinks for myself. It was a popular combination then, but I never liked the flavor. Refreshing citrus dragged down by a heavy undertone of bitter syrup. I took a long pull from the tiny red straw and winced.

I should've gone back to the room with Elaine. My best friend since childhood said what I needed was a trip to the desert. She'd booked us a week at the Cactus Flower Spa in Scottsdale, where we could get massages, sit in steam rooms, soak in mud, and let our tensions melt away with hot-wax pedicures. She said it would break me out of my "funk," as she called it.

I didn't have anything else to do this week.

It was with those sunny thoughts in my head that I saw him. At first I thought it was an accident, my eyes flickering across the square-shaped bar at the same time as his. Blue eyes, strikingly blue because of the way they stood out beneath his dark brow, coupled with collar-length, thick dark hair. He had a beard. I didn't like beards—not even close-trimmed ones like his. He was huge. I could see his muscles from where I sat. His chest strained against the tight, black shirt he wore, and his biceps stretched the sleeves. I preferred smaller men, long and lean model-types.

But he didn't look away. And like a deer caught in headlights, I couldn't either. My breath stilled as my eyes stayed on his, as I waited for him to release me. He would release me. I knew he would. I simply had to wait.

Men in bars were after those baby-faced innocents on the dance floor, not me. They wanted energetic young ones with their tight bodies, high-pitched breasts, and even tighter vaginas. Those were the girls men wanted to fuck. They would scream and moan all night and tell them they were the best ever, the king. I wasn't looking for a king. Still, in the next moment, when the mountain of sex holding my gaze stood and began his slow glide in my direction, all I could think was *maybe...*

I watched as he passed the patrons facing each other, talking and laughing. Some were more animated than others, waving their arms and putting their drinks in peril. They all shone in the yellow lights hidden above, in the recesses of the wooden shelves that held dozens of upside-down glasses in all shapes and sizes. Liquor bottles were arranged on the top shelf. For some reason, though, the lights didn't seem to reach him. Or me. We were in our own secret, shadowy place.

When he rounded the final corner and I could see him in full, my breath caught. My eyes traveled quickly from his broad shoulders to his narrow waist, down his grey pants ending in sleek, black loafers. Just as fast, they were back to his face, and he was in front of me. I'd never been confronted with so much male presence focused on me in my life. He had to be six-two and twice my size.

"Can I buy you a drink?" The low vibration of his voice shot a pleasing charge right between my legs, and my cheeks warmed.

Blinking back to my glass, I poked the half-empty contents with the straw. "I have this," I said, my voice softer and higher in contrast to his.

"But you don't like it." A small smile was on his lips. It made him the slightest bit less intimidating.

"How do you know?"

He leaned against the bar in front of me, bringing his face closer to my level, his body almost touching mine. A faint scent of warm cologne swirled around me, tightening my chest.

"You make a face every time you sip it," he said. "I've been watching you since you walked in with your friend earlier."

My brows drew together. "Why?"

His tongue touched his bottom lip, and my jaw dropped. I quickly closed it, thinking how insane it was the way my body responded to him.

This was not me. I did not fantasize about hooking up with strange men in bars. And a cocky alpha who studied me like I was a frontier landscape he was ready to conquer had never been my type. He probably wanted to tie me up or handcuff me to something. A delicious shiver passed through me at the thought. I put my eyes on my drink.

"Maybe I should introduce myself," he said, holding out a large palm. I stared at it a moment. "Derek."

My eyes lifted to his blue ones, which were still holding me in that intense gaze. He had a small nose and a full mouth. A million pornographic images flooded my brain of that nose nudging into my dark spaces, of that mouth kissing areas long-neglected. That beard scratching the insides of my thighs as I moaned and twisted in white sheets, threading my fingers in his silky hair. I cleared the thickness in my throat, feeling heat everywhere in my body.

"Melissa," I said, placing my noticeably smaller hand in his. His fingers closed over mine, and instead of overwhelming, it felt… right.

"Sweet Melissa," he said with a little grin. The side of his mouth lifting the way it did made me want to kiss him.

"I'm not so sweet," I said, taking my hand back.

"Aren't others supposed to make that judgment?" His eyes never left me as he motioned to the bartender, who immediately came to us. Apparently it wasn't only the perky blondes who got instant service.

"Two glasses of your best cava," Derek said, giving the boy a quick glance before turning back to me.

"Cava?" I did love the crisp, Spanish sparkling wine. Why I hadn't thought to order that instead of my tan cocktail-disaster? "That's sort of a celebratory drink, isn't it?"

"So let's celebrate."

"Did you get a promotion or something?"

He leaned closer, bringing his eyes to my level. My throat tightened, but I didn't move away. "I met you," he said in that low tone I felt in all the right places.

Two slim glasses were placed in front of us, but I wasn't sure I could lift mine without my hand trembling. Derek picked up both and handed one to me. I took it and carefully sipped, watching as he did the same.

"Are you here on business?" I asked, trying to diffuse the ridiculous amount of sexual tension between us. I considered the possibility I was the only one feeling it.

"Banker's conference this week," he said, taking another, longer drink and then setting the glass back on the bar. His muscles fought against the thin fabric restraining them with every movement.

"You're in banking?" I hated the tremor in my voice. It made me sound like a little girl, when I was striving to be an independent woman. A strong woman who was bigger than her past.

For once, I wanted to forget what happened last year. Let it go and be somebody else. I was out of town, in the desert, in a bar being hit on by a gorgeous stranger. Fate was giving me my chance.

"More like upper management," he said, not seeming to notice my distraction. "I'm doing a workshop on international trade and finance tomorrow. You?"

"Spa vacation," I said. "My friend Elaine said it would be a week to change my life. Or at least my outlook."

A little spark hit his eyes, and I bit my lip. Did I just proposition him? Did I want to? It had been a long time since I'd wanted to be close to anyone in that way. Was I brave enough to let him in?

Internally I shook myself. *Yes*. If that was what I wanted, of course I was. I had always been strong before, and I was still strong. I wouldn't let that be taken from me, too.

"Elaine is who you're here with?" he asked.

I nodded, taking another, longer sip. I allowed my mind to release the past and return to better thoughts, like those of him removing that shirt and setting that massive physique free. My desire to see what was under it grew stronger by the minute.

"Will she worry if you're out late?" he asked looking directly into my eyes.

I barely shook my head No. Elaine wouldn't mind. She might even throw a party if I got laid. My breathing had become shallow, and all rational thought was quickly taking a backseat to desire.

"I have a key to the conference room," he said quietly. "There's a small, outdoor patio just off the side. It's very private."

"Why do you have a key?"

"So I can set up in the morning." With that, he straightened up and placed two bills on the bar beside his drink. "Let me show you the desert sky."

"That sounds like it might be dangerous."

His hand touched my arm. "I'll keep you safe."

Safe. It was a word almost erotic to my ears. My eyes traveled from his waist up his torso to his broad shoulders to his lips, past that perfect nose to his darkening eyes. The temperature in my body rose with my gaze.

"You're not safe," I whispered.

"And you're not sweet." His low voice caused my tongue to press against my teeth. I was dying to kiss him. "I'll only do what you let me."

As he said it, I already believed him. His tone was calm, and his eyes said he wasn't lying. Somewhere in my head, the voice of reason was telling me to slow down, but either the cava or the anticipation of what might happen had me floating up, out of my body as I watched him take the slim glass from my hand and help me off my stool. I followed him from the bar, past the dancing girls, and out the narrow exit. Against everything I knew to be prudent, I was doing this.

* * *

Desert heat was still hot. Everyone called it "a dry heat," but it was like opening an oven and getting that first blast right in the face. I'd thought about it when we'd arrived in Arizona earlier today, but now all I was thinking about was the fiery heat blazing through my thighs as Derek held me against the secluded outside wall.

He lifted me as if I weighed no more than a doll, and the hem of my skirt rose all the way up as my legs straddled his waist. His full lips were as soft as they appeared, and they contrasted pleasingly with the scuff of his beard against my skin.

Our mouths opened together, his tongue gently curling with mine, and my hands fumbled to his collar, my fingers threading into his thick hair. Soft and rough forged a fiery trail from my cheek down my jaw to my neck. Little moans rose in my throat with every kiss, and I gasped as my hazy eyes opened to the black sky behind him dotted with thousands of stars. It was a gorgeous view, but I didn't linger on it. The outside patio was secluded—we were completely alone—and my attention was focused on the progress of his mouth as he explored every part of my neck and shoulders with his lips and tongue.

He unzipped the back of my dress, allowing the sleeves to fall down around my elbows as his mouth covered the swell of my breasts. My nipples tingled for his touch, and the only sounds were my rapid panting punctuated by little noises of pleasure. Electricity flew through my body, warming the space between my legs, and I was surrounded by the woodsy scent of his cologne mingled with the growing smell of sex.

His mouth returned to mine, and my fingers dug into his flesh. He was firm and tight, and the way he rocked me against the wall, the swell in his jeans massaging my clit, had me on the brink of orgasm. I wanted him inside me. Desperately.

"Take off your shirt." My voice was a hoarse whisper I didn't recognize. It sounded almost animal.

He lowered me to the ground, his blue eyes now dark navy, as he quickly grabbed the back of his shirt and whipped it over his head. Energy flooded my core then surged low into my pelvis. His smooth skin was the color of coffee with cream, and a whisper of hair covered the top of his chest. I reached out to run my fingers slowly down the cut, muscular lines on his stomach, and he shuddered slightly before catching my hips and pulling me up against him again.

My legs went back around his waist. I was still in my black push-up bra, but I wanted everything off. I wanted my bare breasts pressed against that gorgeous chest. I quickly reached around and unhooked it, slipping my arms from the straps as his mouth covered one hard nipple. Low noises came from his throat as he kissed and gently bit. It was a tense, almost primitive demand, his hands tightening their hold on my ass. A trembling moan ached from my throat. The coarse fabric of the balcony curtain was against my bare back, and his musky scent almost pushed me over the edge.

"I'm clean, but I'll use protection," he said in a rough voice.

It was a foregone conclusion—we were having sex. Only my thong stood between me and what was coming. His mouth traveled back to mine, but I placed my palms lightly on his cheeks, holding his dark eyes for a moment.

"Why me?" I gasped. I had to ask. I wouldn't be me if I didn't.

His hands squeezed my bare bottom. "I love long dark curls and blue eyes."

It was enough. Our mouths crashed together again, and his fingers slid inside me. Two thick digits pressed in and out, exploring what was wet with need. My mouth broke from his and I moaned against his shoulder, gripping his waist with my thighs as his fingers left me and quickly worked below his waist. The sharp metallic clang of a belt buckle was quickly followed by the sound of a wrapper tearing.

I held my breath, my heartbeat, everything. My mouth opened, and he slid into me with a loud groan.

"Oh my god," I gasped. He was huge. I'd never been so full. It was amazing and erotic, and I was about to come. High whimpers gasped from my throat as my orgasm grew stronger, his enormous shaft stretched and massaged every erogenous zone between my legs.

I lay my head back against the wall and let go, savoring the sensation. I was weightless in his arms. He lifted me up and down against him in perfect rhythm, and the tightness in my belly grew stronger. Stronger. More high-pitched whimpers came from me, now joined by his low groans. Every muscle in my body tightened, and then... exploded. He bucked me hard as I cried out loud. My legs shuddered with the intensity of my orgasm.

Two more deep thrusts and he was still, gasping, his face pressed into the crook of my neck. We stayed that way several moments. I didn't want him to pull out. The spasms of my orgasm were still tightening the muscles inside me, and with every movement, residual flickers of delicious energy touched me. I held him with my eyes closed. I'd never been fucked like that in my life. I was actually wondering if I'd ever fucked at all after that.

His hips thrust up slowly, gently, and I whimpered again. "I love that sound," he murmured against my neck. "So fucking hot."

His lips pressed more burning kisses against my shoulder, and my nipples tingled at the light brush of his chest hair. All of my senses were heightened as he wrapped huge arms around my waist in an embrace. Slowly rocking his hips again, I tightened my thighs. My orgasm was still fading, and I pressed my face against his neck. Every time my inner muscles would spasm around his cock he'd give me another, gentle thrust and I'd make a little noise, until at last my body seemed satiated. The trembling subsided, and I could think again.

He lifted me and slid out, lowering me to my shaky legs. "Thank you," he whispered. My forehead rested against his cheek, and I felt almost as if it were a dream.

"Thank you," I repeated, stepping back carefully. I located my bra and put it on before pulling the sleeves of my dress back over my shoulders. I slid the zipper up slowly as I watched him restore his pants, fasten his buckle.

I couldn't take my eyes off him. I'd never done anything like this in my life, and I was at a total loss — what now? Did we shake hands and walk away? We'd already thanked each other, another thing I'd never done — thanked a man for sex. Of course, this guy had completely earned it.

He stopped before putting on his shirt and took a step toward me, blue gaze catching mine. "We'll both be here all week?" he said, and the intoxicating scent of his woodsy cologne flooded my senses.

I nodded, knowing what he was getting at.

"I'll be tied up with meetings and networking during the day," he said. "But every night, I'll go to that bar."

I studied him. A one-night stand was one thing, but a one-week stand? With him? After that? It felt like a recipe for disaster. It was going to be hard enough to move past what just happened between us, but adding five more days on top of it? I might never recover.

"I'll be on some regimen at the spa, I guess," I said, my eyes never leaving his.

He put one palm on the wall beside my face and lowered his. Our mouths were a breath apart. "I hope I'll see you again."

I almost melted on the spot. My eyes blinked slowly. "It's a nice bar. And I like cava."

That small grin lifted the side of his mouth, and he kissed me lightly before straightening up and slipping the shirt back over his head. His hair was now in messy waves, and I wanted to run my fingers through them again. Instead, I stepped into my wedge stacks and took the hand he offered as he led me through the dark room and out the side door. He paused to lock it and then turned to face me.

"Shall I escort you back to your room?" he asked.

I shook my head no. I didn't want him knowing my room number yet, although he could easily ask the front desk for it, I supposed.

"Then *adieu*," he said, lifting my hand and kissing it. "Til tomorrow night."

I watched until he released me, then I turned and walked as steadily as possible to the exit, to the spa side of the resort where we were staying.

CHAPTER 2 – NOT AVAILABLE IN ANY WAY

The tenderness in my thigh muscles combined with a feeling of calm satisfaction deep inside me were the first indicators what happened last night was not a dream. The next was the scent of his woodsy cologne in my long, dark hair. I lifted a lock and pressed it to my nose, closing my eyes and enjoying his warm scent. It triggered a damp flicker of memory between my legs.

For several long moments, I lay in the soft hotel bed, replaying how last night even happened. Elaine and I had gone to the bar straight from checking in and dropping our bags in our room. We were tired after a long two-days of travel that started with me in Maryland and her in North Carolina. Our first night was spent in Atlanta, where we'd shared a room and stayed awake almost all night talking and catching up. Then we'd flown cross-country to Arizona, and even though it felt early, the day of switching airplanes, running through airports, and hauling bags after our late night had us both tired. I was doubly weighed-down by the problems I'd left at home. One drink, and Elaine wanted to sleep. But I'd wanted to have another. I needed the alcohol to deaden the nonstop pain of my shattered life.

And then he'd appeared.

Images of me pressed against the patio wall, his huge cock thrusting into me, both of us groaning loudly as we came flashed across my memory, and my eyes flew wide. I blinked at the ceiling, thinking about how insane that was. How stupid and potentially dangerous. Clearly the last year hadn't only left me depressed, it also left me engaging in out-of-character and unbelievably risky behavior.

A shiver of longing moved through me at the memory of being held against his firm chest. I sighed. Risky, yes, but how incredibly hot and amazing he was. And he didn't hurt me. He was actually very attentive. He held me all the way to the end, and he even thanked me. My nose wrinkled as a sneaky grin passed over my lips. I thanked him back. What was *that* about?

Then I thought about tonight. Him at the bar waiting. Would I go back? My immediate answer was *yes*, but was that smart? I had a hot memory of the most incredible sex of my life. Maybe it was best to preserve it and not tempt fate with something I'd only leave behind in one short week.

"What time did you get in last night?" Elaine stepped out of the bathroom interrupting my thoughts. She wore one of the thick, white terry robes, and she patted her damp, blonde hair with an equally plush towel.

"I don't remember," I said, rolling onto my stomach. "It wasn't too late. Are we hitting the spa today?"

"I've got us scheduled for massages at eleven, then we'll have lunch in the quiet room, then we can hang around the deck pool. I've heard the waiters there are panty-dropping hot."

I smiled, thinking they'd have to be off the charts to top what I'd had last night. "Sound like the perfect, relaxing day."

Elaine sat on the edge of the bed, drawing her brows together. "You look pretty relaxed right now. What'd you do after I left?"

"Just had another drink. People-watched."

She pressed her lips together in disbelief, but she didn't pursue it. "You'd better get moving if you're going to shower first."

"Don't they just cover us in oil anyway?" I pushed myself to a sitting position.

"That's part of the detoxification."

"Then I'll just do a quick rinse and shower after." I hated the residue of oil on my skin all day, although in the desert, it would probably be a welcome relief from the dryness.

Elaine's tone grew serious. "Have you heard anything?"

My troubles at home came threatening back, and I looked down at my hands as I shook my head. "I emailed everyone that we were out of town for the week. Taking a mental health break. It should be enough."

She exhaled and patted the top of my hands. "You're doing the right thing."

My eyes flickered to hers, and tears threatened. She was the first person to voice support for me since the ordeal began, and it meant everything. I scooted forward to hug her, and she hugged me with a deep inhale. Instantly she jerked and pulled back, studying my face with narrowed eyes.

"What's that smell?"

My face flushed bright red, and I pulled away. She caught my long hair and pulled it to her nose. "That's a *very* nice man-scent if I've ever smelled one."

I shook my head. "I don't know what it is. Just some old cologne."

"Not *your* old cologne. What else happened after you finished your drink?"

Jumping off the bed, I quickly grabbed yoga pants, a bra, and a tank before stepping into the bathroom.

"Melissa?" Elaine was hot on my trail. I pushed the door closed, but she caught it in a crack.

"I just slow-danced with some guy," I lied, coiling my hair into a knot at the top of my head. "It was nothing."

"Just slow danced? He wears a lot of cologne, then." Her voice rose. "Unless it was more like dirty-dancing."

She had no idea. I turned on the shower, holding my hand under the spray to test the temperature. "Seriously, let's just drop it," I said. "You know I'm not interested in meeting anyone. And anyway, I'm not available."

"Maybe not emotionally available."

I pulled the glass shower door closed. "Not available in any way."

* * *

Warm, oil-coated hands slid down the length of my back, pushing all the pain down and out through my torso. I lay on a crisp white sheet atop the firm massage table, entirely naked except for a second sheet draped

22

across my bum. Water trickled softly in the desktop fountain, creating a relaxing ambience, and soft beach noises played on a track overhead. The room was dark, and incense lightly filled the air.

I'd never been one of those people who moaned and groaned through massages, but I was on the verge today. When the female masseuse began working on my thighs, the fresh ache from last night's unexpected workout flooded my mind with memories of Derek. I wanted to see him again. I wanted his huge fullness inside me again, stretching me and coaxing every sensitive spot. I wanted to shoot over the edge in another incredible orgasm with him. But what I'd said to Elaine was true. I was *not* available.

Still, he hadn't asked me for a commitment, and from what I could tell, he wasn't looking for anything. One week, he'd said. We could share one week of pleasure, couldn't we? It could be our little secret. Or was I too old-school for that?

The masseuse gently helped me roll over, keeping the second sheet over my private parts. Her expert hands moved to my shoulders, pushing the stress away as her strong thumbs circled, traveling up my neck to my scalp. I remembered the sensation of Derek's lips, his scratchy beard traveling down my neck to my breasts. Moisture was growing between my legs, and I could feel my nipples harden. Luckily the sheet was doubled thick across my chest.

The masseuse gently placed her palms flat against my shoulders.

"Rest until you're ready to come out, Ms. Jones," she said softly before leaving me alone in the small, dark room.

With my eyes closed, I remembered his touch. My hands were flat on the table beside me as I lay on my back. I remembered him gripping my bare buttocks, squeezing them as he rocked me against the curtain, covering my body with his. I remembered pulling off my bra and his ravenous kisses, his gentle bites. I remembered his thick fingers pushing inside me, and instinctively, my hands slipped to my now-tingling clitoris, massaging circles over the sensitive spot. With my eyes closed, I felt his enormous cock push inside me, and in that instant, my body shook with the orgasm I'd provoked. My legs trembled, and I pressed my lips together to keep from moaning loudly.

I wanted him again. Oh, god, even if I wasn't available in any way, I wanted him again so badly.

* * *

Out by the pool, I lay back in the lounge chair, hiding behind dark sunglasses. My hair still had residual oils in it from the massage, but I hadn't washed it. Behind the magazine I held, I casually lifted a lock and sniffed his warm cologne lingering in it.

In my head, I scolded myself. What was I doing? I had to stop this immediately. I slammed the magazine down and stripped off the terry robe I was wearing. In my red bikini, I was still mistaken for being younger than thirty. My stomach was flat, and my skin was tight. No cellulite on my thighs, and my favorite exercise, running, kept my derriere lifted. I'd always just called it good genes, although this last year of pain had taken the once-happy glow from my eyes. My former, easy smile seemed permanently a thing of the past. It was a big part of what made observers think I was younger, and now it was gone. Stolen from me.

Stepping up on the diving board, I fixed my chin. I strode across the plank and did a perfect jackknife dive into the pool, allowing the cooling water to wash away the final remnants of last night. I was *not* available in *any* way.

* * *

Twilight in the desert was a beautiful sight.

Elaine and I held glasses of wine as we watched the huge sky turn from blue to pink to dim purple, the fire-pit in the center of our circle of lounge chairs keeping us from getting chilled. As always, I was amazed how the temperature could drop from the 100s to the 70s so fast.

"Wasn't today perfect?" my friend asked as she stretched out, covering herself with one of the complimentary Indian-designed blankets folded across the backs of each chair.

"Perfectly relaxing," I agreed, taking another sip of my wine and forbidding my mind from drifting to the small bar situated between the two halves of the sprawling resort.

He would be there waiting, I was sure of it. And I wondered what reason he would tell himself when I never appeared. He was an amazing lay, and I knew he knew it. I'd been clearly satisfied last night. I took a deep breath and exhaled, drinking another, longer gulp of wine. I couldn't imagine what he'd think.

"Still nothing from home?" Elaine asked, studying my profile.

A missed call had been on my phone, and I'd listened to Sloan's message, demanding to know where I was as I fought the pain his voice now twisted in my gut. I was making a mistake, he kept saying. I was being too hasty, too judgmental. Every message was a lecture in why I shouldn't trust my instincts. I pushed his words and their meaning behind me.

"Nothing important," I said.

"You know, Mel, we've been friends for years." She sat forward in her chair, tightening the blanket around her shoulders. "Something's different today. Won't you tell me what it is?"

My eyes flickered to hers, and for a moment, I considered telling her about the amazing man who'd appeared at the bar last night. Who'd only wanted me, even with all the shiny, happy options twisting and giggling on the dance floor. He'd singled me out. Crossed the bar to be with me.

With damaged me.

Even in the old days when I was whole, no man had ever approached me that way. All of my relationships got serious after the groundwork of friendship had been laid. Either I'd had a project with a man, and after our personalities had meshed, we'd grown into dating. Or even back in college—I'd been in clubs, socializing for weeks with guys before they'd asked me out. It wasn't that I wasn't attractive, and I'd had my share of sexual encounters. I was just never the girl men sought out from across a room crowded with other options.

Until last night.

I felt special, but at the same time, it made me hesitant. Was it possible I was singled out because I was an easy mark? A woman alone, clearly unhappy would easily fall victim to the charms of such a handsome seducer.

Again, these were the not-so sunny thoughts my now-cynical brain conjured when I thought of myself and love. Would I ever be open again or would my heart forever be searching for the hidden truth, the other side of the coin?

"I'm tired," I exhaled, unfolding my legs from beneath me. "I think I'll turn in early tonight if that's okay."

With her question unanswered, Elaine frowned as she watched me rise. "You've been dealt some heavy disappointment this past year," she said. "Try not to give up, okay?"

I nodded, leaning forward and kissing her forehead. "Don't stay up too late. Mani-pedis in the morning?"

She smiled and nodded. "The calf massage will make you come in your chair, from what I've heard."

I laughed. "You've heard a lot about this place."

"Bulletin board reviews. They're unexpectedly erotic."

CHAPTER 3 – THE ADDITIONAL OPTION

Calf and foot massages kept pedicures at the top of my list of all-time favorite spa-treatments. It was the one procedure that almost made me forget my "silent spa" etiquette. Holding the magazine, I leaned my head back in the chair and closed my eyes. The gentle kneading of my tired lower leg muscles had me conceding to Elaine — this week very well could break me out of my funk. Even without the Derek encounter.

My eyelids drooped with fatigue. Last night, I'd tossed and turned for an hour before finally falling into a restless slumber. I kept seeing his blue eyes turned dark navy with desire. For me. The thought made me shiver. Until 2 a.m., all I could do was wonder if he was still there. How long would he wait? Was I making a huge mistake?

Elaine returned about an hour later, and my sterner nature prevailed. I remained in my own bed, in my own room the entire night. Today, she was a little bleary herself.

"What kept you out so late?" I asked, wondering if she might've had her own decadent encounter.

"Fell asleep on the lounger by the fire pit," she said, propping her newly buffed and polished feet on the empty tub near mine. The clinician had finished my massage and was now scrubbing my heels with a pumice stone. "It's so gorgeous here, I might never go home."

I thought of Baltimore and how I hadn't wanted to move there a year ago. I'd lived just outside Wilmington, on the North Carolina coast for years, and I loved it there. But Sloan had insisted a change of scenery would help us, and when his father died, he needed to be closer to his family's business.

Since I'd gone freelance with my marketing work, and we were moving to another bustling, urban location, there was no reason to fight the move. Other than I loved my hometown. Elaine was there, along with all my old friends.

"I know this is only Day 2, my friend, but I have a confession to make," she said, giving me a serious look. My brow creased. I couldn't imagine what she was about to tell me. "I can't eat another meal of raw foods."

I snorted a laugh, rubbing my forehead with my hand. "What did you have in mind?"

"Let's sneak over to the dark side and order a burger in the main restaurant."

I hesitated. Crossing from the spa resort to the main hotel would increase my chances of running into Derek again. But if he were tied up in conference meetings like he claimed, it was possible we could get in and out without being seen. Still, the thought of bumping into him after my no-show last night made me uneasy.

"Maybe we should just drive into town," I suggested. "I think there's some big thing going on next door and it's probably crowded."

She played with the massage-chair controller while she waited, and didn't notice my worried expression. "A banker's convention," she said, not looking up. "Can you imagine a bigger snooze-fest? Probably a bunch of accountants."

"Probably," I said, remembering Derek saying he was in upper management. "But I'm sure there are other executives there as well, don't you think?"

She glanced up at me then. "Sounds interesting. Maybe we can meet someone and have a little bonus treatment. Some sexual healing?"

"What about Brian?" Elaine's boyfriend back home had been a fixture in her life for years.

She shook her head. "That book's coming to a close, I think."

I sat up quickly, "You never told me this. What happened?"

"Nothing." Her lips pressed together. "And that's just it. I don't feel anything toward him. It's been five years. *Five years!* And I still can't imagine marrying him." She released an exhale. "Sadly, it seems he is not my one true love."

Reaching across the space, I clasped her hand. "I'm so sorry, Lainey. I had no idea. I've been so self-absorbed."

Her hand covered mine with a squeeze. "Please. You've had damn good reasons to be preoccupied. And honestly, I can't even work up the energy to cry over it. I just want to be done. I think he feels the same."

I shook my head, but she winked. "So let's find something new, yes? A desert memento?"

The clinician was finished with my feet and slipping the thin foam flip-flops against my now-smooth soles. "At least let me get changed first."

* * *

The mid-day Arizona heat swirled around us as we walked from the spa lobby across the short, circular drive to the huge, main complex. The resort consisted of three large towers and was all bronze glass, blending nicely with the terrain. Palm trees lined the drive and rocky fountains stood in front of each entrance. I'd slipped on a black skirt and beige tank top and pulled my hair into a low, side ponytail that sent dark curls spilling down my chest. Elaine was wearing a little green dress that made her green eyes glow, and her straight blonde hair hung loose down her back. We both wore flip-flops to preserve our bright salmon pedicures.

The restaurant was crowded as I'd expected, and I tried not to appear to be scanning every face for signs of him. So far, he didn't seem to be here. As we waited for the hostess to return and seat us, a fellow about our age walked up and requested a table.

He was handsome, with honey blond hair and hazel eyes. He wore khaki shorts and topsiders without socks, and I noticed his biceps were well-toned. He also seemed to have a defined chest under his short-sleeved polo. I had to wonder when the banking industry had gotten so sexy. Elaine noticed him, too, and smiled.

The second hostess marked the plastic board in front of her and handed him a square pager. He stepped back and joined us staring into the enormous tropical fish tank that separated the waiting area from part of the dining room.

My friend glanced at him. "Here for the convention?" she said, switching into full flirt-mode.

His eyes lit when he saw how pretty she was, and he turned to face us. "Yeah," he said. "You?"

Elaine shook her head. "We're here for the spa."

He glanced over her shoulder at me and nodded with a smile. I smiled back, and he returned his attention to her.

"I'm Elaine," she said, twisting a lock of her hair around a finger as she leaned into him. "And this is my best friend Melissa."

"Patrick Knight," he said, shaking her hand and taking a step closer as well. "Nice to meet you both."

"Are you waiting for someone, Patrick?" The defining difference between Elaine and me was her complete lack of hesitancy around men. Of course, she'd never been given a reason to hesitate.

"Just my business partner," he said. "We were at the gym earlier, and he's still in his room."

"Is he a banker, too?"

"Nah." Patrick had a charming smile with straight, white teeth. "Neither of us are, really. More freelance consultants. Knight and Alexander."

He handed her a business card, and she took it. But Elaine's eyes moved from the cream rectangle to Patrick's torso. "That sounds fascinating," she said, allowing her eyes to travel slowly up his chest. "I'd love to hear more about your work."

He cleared his throat, obviously appreciating her admiration of his body. "Why don't you ladies join us?"

"Oh, we can't," I quickly jumped in. I wasn't ready to meet yet another banking convention attendee. "We've got a treatment this afternoon, so we're kind of on a schedule."

"Dinner, then," he insisted.

"Perfect," Elaine cut me off before I could block her action again. "What time?"

"Eight o'clock? Here?" Patrick once again had Elaine's hand in his.

"See you then," she said.

The hostess appeared, perfectly timed to escort us to our table, and as we followed her, I carefully scanned the large dining area for his face.

"Yum!" Elaine caught my arm and leaned into my ear, speaking in a low voice. "Wouldn't it be lovely to add him to our treatment schedule?"

"Hmm… I think my schedule's full," I said, taking a seat at our table.

I cautiously glanced behind me after giving my drink order, but I still didn't see any sign of him. As far as I could tell, he wasn't having lunch here.

"Maybe this Alexander guy is equally hot," she said with a wink.

I shrugged, sipping my iced tea. "Wouldn't matter."

The corner of her mouth curled up. "We'll see tonight. This might be the additional option you need."

Her words provoked a little laugh from me. She had no idea what additional option I'd already had, and I doubted this Alexander person would be able to top it. That flash of memory caused me to inspect the restaurant once more. Not seeing him, my stomach unclenched enough for me to eat our non-cleansing lunch of cheeseburgers and fries.

Chapter 4 – Special Forces

Even though I had no interest in Patrick's partner, when I saw Elaine putting on her strapless, ruched-top dress, I pulled mine out of the closet as well. They were perfect for the weather—handkerchief print, knee-length, and flowing. We'd bought them in the spa store together. Elaine's was black with purple swirling designs, and mine was a bright red with hot pink accents. We each had a glass of the in-room white wine as we made up our faces and dressed.

Using a large brush, I dusted translucent powder over my nose and up my temples to my forehead where my eyes landed on a faded pink scar at my hairline. My lips pressed together, and that old pain twisted inside my chest. I lowered the brush as my hand fumbled to my wine glass. Taking a long sip, I waited a moment for the feelings to pass.

It was over, I reminded myself. That part of my life had ended. I had put all the wheels in motion before I even stepped foot on the plane to come here—before I'd even known I was coming here. Now it was time to let healing take place. I had to let go of what had happened to me and move forward.

A few cleansing breaths, and my control began easing back. Tapping my finger against the pot of concealer, I touched the flesh-toned makeup over the thin pink line, and it was gone. For a split second I imagined a concealer for heart scars. Instead I shook my head. *Over*, I repeated in my brain. Another deep inhale, and I was ready to emerge from the bathroom.

Elaine was leaning down, fastening the buckle on her sandal when I walked out. Her straight, blonde hair spilled like silk around her shoulders, and when she stood, we both caught our breaths. "You're beautiful!" we practically said simultaneously. Then we laughed.

"Oh, Mel," my best friend said, coming over and wrapping her arms around me. "It's moments like these when I know you're going to be okay. Just give it time."

I nodded hugging her back and pressing my lips against her temple. The clean scent of the spa-signature cactus flower toiletries flooded my senses. It was a relaxing smell, and I imagined if she disappeared with Patrick, he'd love it.

"I'm doing my best," I said. "I know holding onto the past is the worst thing anyone can do."

My psychologist mother would be the first to have me on her couch reciting these axioms to me if I dared let her know what had happened. As it stood, only three people knew the whole story—me, him, and Elaine, the closest person I had to a sister. It was a cliché not to tell anyone, but I didn't have the energy or the willingness to involve the authorities. And I didn't want everyone knowing my tragic tale.

It was finished. I'd made my decision, and I was putting it behind me. My instincts said to cut my losses, cut all ties, and move on. I'd made my first step before leaving Baltimore. This trip was the second, and when I got back, I'd take the third.

What happened with Derek might be extended as part of me cutting ties, my declaration of freedom from my past... But more likely it was just a blip on the radar screen. An incredible distraction, that was now through.

Walking to the restaurant, the dry breeze blew our hair back. I lifted the weight of my dark locks around one shoulder and linked arms with my friend.

"We should do trips like this more often," she said, looking up at the desert sky. "It's wonderful being together, and there's nothing stopping us now. I had a long talk with Brian this afternoon, and that's done. Clean break. We're both free agents."

My arm tightened on hers, and I pulled her to a stop. "Are you okay?"

She nodded and smiled. "It really was over before I even called you about coming here. It's sad, but I promise, I'm so relieved we've finally made it official. It was turning into the longest goodbye on record."

"Was Brian part of the reason you planned this spa retreat?"

She pulled me, and we started walking again. "Only a small part. I knew how much you needed it, too. I could hear it in your voice every time we talked."

Another deep, cleansing breath. "Well, I think your idea sounds fantastic. Let's plan our next trip as soon as we get back."

"Will you be coming home to the shore now?" her delicate eyebrows pulled together.

I bit my lip and nodded. "Definitely. The best part about working freelance is it goes with me anywhere. And I have lots of contacts in Wilmington."

"Oh, that makes me so happy," she beamed, doing a little skip. "We are definitely planning our next trip. What do you think? Is Thanksgiving too soon?"

I laughed as we entered the restaurant, glad I'd had that glass of wine. I was at ease and far less nervous about accidentally bumping into Derek this time. Elaine told the hostess we were with Patrick and Mr. Alexander as I hung back beside the aquarium.

When she motioned for us to follow her, my friend clasped the crook of my arm and leaned in to my ear. "If this is the 'Mr. Alexander' I found online, it should be a very interesting dinner."

I shook my head and smiled. Her nonstop online investigations were becoming an entertaining distraction.

"Why?" I whispered, picturing a grey-haired old gentleman with a name like *Mr. Alexander*.

Just then, my eyes found Patrick sitting at a large round table in the back. It was covered in a crisp, white tablecloth, and a vase of bright yellow sunflowers formed the centerpiece, corresponding with the gold décor.

Elaine's words were just meeting my ears when my breath disappeared from my throat. "Derek Alexander is a leader in the field of online investigation. And he's hot as hell."

My brain scrambled as his blue eyes caught mine, and I involuntarily took a step back. "Oh," I said softly, feeling my chest tighten at the sight of him.

There he sat, wearing a light-blue, short-sleeved polo that stretched across that chest that had been pressed against mine less than forty-eight hours ago.

"What's wrong?" Elaine said, stepping between me and the table, studying my face.

I shook my head, attempting to breathe normally. "It's nothing!" My voice was too high, and behind her, I saw his dark form rise to his full height. But I couldn't look. I was afraid I might faint.

"Elaine!" Patrick's happy voice cut through my whirlwind of emotions. "You look great."

She beamed, turning quickly to him. "Thanks," she said, stepping around to catch Patrick's hand and leaving me to face the man I'd stood up the night before.

Derek's eyes flickered with a hint of amusement and definite satisfaction. "Melissa," he said in that low voice that rattled me to my core.

I blinked down to the table. "I didn't know..." Actually, I had no idea what to say at this point. Nothing in my life up to now had prepared me for this situation.

Elaine stepped back around to extend her hand to him. "You must be Mr. Alexander," she smiled.

Derek stepped forward to take her hand, then leaned in to kiss her cheek briefly. "Derek, please."

Elaine's eyes widened. "I love your cologne," she said, glancing at me with knowing eyes. "What is it?"

Heat flooded my cheeks. Again, I was having difficulty breathing.

Derek laughed. "You know, I'm not sure. I transferred it to one of those plastic travel bottles for airport security a while back, and now I can't remember."

"It's so familiar," Elaine said. "Almost like something I smelled yesterday..."

He shrugged. "I rarely wear cologne, but I liked the scent. Fresh, not too overpowering."

"But lingering," my friend said.

She wouldn't stop, and I wanted to die as I pulled out the chair directly in front of me. It formed an awkward arrangement—Elaine sitting next to Patrick, Derek across from me a few chairs down from them. A waiter appeared ready for our drink orders, and Derek immediately ordered a bottle of cava for the table.

"It's a favorite, I believe," he said, turning his blue eyes on me.

I glanced down to my lap, attempting to stop the flood of images of us together on the secret patio. Every time I looked at his face, I remembered the brush of his lips against mine, the scratch of his beard, the sensation of his chest hair against my bare nipples. I was certain the entire room could see me flush or at the very least, how fast I was breathing.

"So tell me," Elaine said, "Are you *the* Derek Alexander, top internet piracy detective, ex-Marine, and former cop?"

"*Retired Marine* and *police officer* are preferred," he said with a wink as the waiter appeared with a dark-green bottle. "And I'm not sure I'm the top, but I am hired to speak at conferences quite a bit."

"Fascinating," Elaine said, and I could feel her eyes moving to me.

I continued to study the place setting in front of me. Detective? Marine? Former cop? Great. All of those labels only complicated my situation.

The cork popped and four glasses of sparkling wine were served. Derek lifted his. "To the little things," he said.

"Meeting up with pleasant acquaintances," Elaine said, lifting her glass.

I brought mine to my lips and took a long drink.

"So you didn't tell me what you do," Patrick jumped in with his sunny voice. Everything about him was happy, and I figured Elaine could do much worse for a spa-vacation fling. Or transition guy. Unlike me, who only seemed destined for trouble.

"Mel's a freelance marketer," she said, nodding at me. "I teach middle school."

"What?" Patrick laughed. "That's the worst age ever!"

Elaine joined him in laughter. "They're just a misunderstood bunch. All raging hormones. But they want to be loved and accepted just like everyone else."

I could feel Derek's intense gaze on me, and I didn't dare look at him. Instead I faced Patrick, a far less intimidating table mate. "So you work in internet security?"

Patrick's hazel eyes twinkled. "That's right, and don't worry. We've already done complete background checks on both you lovely ladies."

My throat tightened, but Elaine laughed loudly. "Liar! You don't even know our last names."

"You got me," he smiled, taking a drink of cava. "But I will after tonight."

"Maybe I'll keep you guessing," she said.

Their easy banter was making my head hurt. Especially in view of Derek's continued silence. I took another drink, finishing my glass.

"So if all the bad guys are virtual now, why are you two so buff?" Elaine said, touching Patrick's biceps lightly. "I'm pretty sure Derek's arm is the size of my thigh!"

My eyes flickered to his upper arm, and I remembered how easily he lifted me against him, as if I weighed no more than a doll. My cheeks heated at the memory.

"Occasionally Big D has to use intimidation tactics," Patrick said as if revealing an insider secret.

"Big D?" Elaine's nose wrinkled.

I could hear the smile in Derek's low voice. "It's a joke."

The pressure was too much. I stood, placing my napkin beside my empty plate and now-empty cava flute. "Excuse me," I said softly.

Elaine frowned up at me. "Mel? Are you okay?"

She started to rise, but I held out my hand. "Please stay. I just... I need to go. I'll have dinner in the room."

"But you don't have a key!"

"I'll get one from the front desk. Please... just stay." I turned and hastened to the restaurant exit.

Elaine spoke again, and the low sound of male voices joined hers, but I didn't stop. My heart was flying, and I was out the door, fast-walking through the convention center hall in less than a minute.

I'd intended to exit the way we'd come in, but somehow, I'd gotten turned around. Now I was headed in the direction of the small bar from our very first night. Between me and it were three signs for men, women, and the large "family" bathroom. I paused, trying to remember the quickest way back to the spa side of the resort. Just then, I felt a presence approaching quickly. I started to go, but Derek's voice stopped me.

"Wait," he said, touching my arm.

I turned so abruptly, he bumped into me, catching me in his strong embrace, his familiar woodsy scent all around me. "Oh," I said, clutching his solid arms, looking up into his intense blue eyes. Energy rushed through me so hard, I was sure he could see it. I almost felt like I could see it reflected in his own eyes.

"Here," he said glancing around quickly before pulling me into the family bathroom.

I only had a moment to observe how very clean it was before he had me against the wall, pinned by his huge physique.

"You never came." His voice was a low, husky whisper. "I waited all night."

My hands rested on his chest, and heat flamed through me with every heartbeat. My eyes traveled up, up, up to his. They were darkened now, and I was certain he was thinking the same thing as me. He remembered how fantastically our bodies came together two nights ago. I barely registered him reaching out to lock the door.

"I'm sorry," was all I could say.

"When you walked in the restaurant tonight... god, you're so beautiful." He spoke against my skin as his lips pressed into my brow, his beard roughing my closed eyelids. "Are you feeling bad?"

"No," I managed to say despite the heat surging through me as his lips moved to my temple. "I... didn't think I could eat."

"Good," he said in a thick voice before covering my mouth with his. Mine opened quickly, drawing him in. Our tongues entwined before his lips moved to my jaw then down my neck. "I thought about you all day." His breath whispered across my skin, and I couldn't stop a surge of desire low in my stomach. "Will you let me have you here?"

"Yes," I barely spoke, and he dropped to his knees.

He gathered the thin fabric of my dress, shoving it

up to my waist as he caught the side of my thong with his thumb. Large, strong hands gripped my inner thighs, opening them, and his nose touched the crease in my leg as his tongue explored my now-wet folds. A whimper trembled from my throat. It was the exact fantasy I'd had in the bar, and he pulled back, pressing his mouth against my thigh.

"I had to hear that sound again." His voice was a sexy vibration against my skin, his beard scratching my charged, sensitive areas. I shuddered in his strong hands that held me as if I weighed nothing at all.

His mouth returned to my clit, and his tongue began making slow strokes punctuated by little sucks. My head dropped back with a moan, eyes closed, as my hips rotated in time with his movements.

"Oooh, god," I sighed, threading my fingers into his thick, dark hair, never wanting him to stop. My back arched against the cold stone wall, and all I knew was his mouth, his tongue, tasting me, teasing me to the very edge. Pressure grew hot and tight low in my belly, tighter with every pull of his mouth. My hips bucked as my orgasm began, and another high-pitched whimper escaped my throat. My shudders were uncontrollable as I came.

I was still finishing when he stood quickly, fumbled with his pants a moment before I heard the familiar tearing sound, the clink of a belt buckle. In one swift movement, he lifted me easily, then slid me down, thrusting into my dripping-wet passage, filling me completely like before, stretching and massaging every place that ached for him. We both groaned loudly, and he pushed into me again, harder. My hands fumbled to the collar of his shirt, down his back, pulling the fabric up, desperate to feel his skin.

He groaned low as I managed to get his polo higher, the strapless top of my dress now pushed down around my waist, my bare breasts tingling for his touch. Our skin met, and I moaned with satisfaction.

"Fuck," his low voice groaned as his hands gripped my butt, moving me up and down his shaft in the most amazing rhythm.

My second orgasm was building rapidly as his large cock moved in and out repeatedly. His mouth covered mine, and the small whimpers coming from my throat were like fuel to his fire. Our pace increased. The tightness in my stomach grew more intense, and my nails dug into his skin. My heart was beating so hard, and my brain had switched to repeating one phrase, *Don't stop. Don't stop.*

Finally the tightness reached its peak and burst through me—shaking my thighs again and making me moan.

"Fuck me," he groaned, thrusting hard. "You're so fucking hot."

"Derek," I whispered against his ear, and he let out a breath.

"Say it again," he ground out, lifting me and slamming me hard against his hips, his rock-hard cock filling me entirely.

"Oh, god," I cried. "Derek!"

With that, he pushed me against the wall, banging into me three swift times before holding the fourth so deep inside me, I felt his heartbeat pounding. A shiver moved through his body, and he groaned soft and low.

We didn't move for several moments. He only held me against him, both of us panting hard.

Our location came seeping back to me through the delirium of love-making. We were in a bathroom in a five-star hotel fucking our brains out. This was nuts. I gently pushed against his arms, and he released me. As I lowered my legs, I adjusted my thong. I slid the top of my dress back to its proper location and I smoothed my hair.

I turned to the sink, unsure if I felt insane or fantastic. My legs trembled from exertion and sensation. One thing I couldn't deny, my fears of ruining the memory of our perfect first time were unfounded. Our second time was even hotter. I turned on the water and touched my fingers under the stream as I listened to him straightening his clothes.

In a moment he was back behind me, bending down to wrap his chiseled arms around my waist and whispering in my ear like before, "Thank you." Then he kissed the top of my shoulder.

No man had ever thanked me for sex like this, and I wasn't sure if I liked it or if it made me feel like a call girl. I decided to go with the first option. He wasn't offering me money, after all, just gratitude. It was a gratitude I shared. He fucked me better than anybody had in my entire life.

My eyes met his in the mirror. "Thank you," I said back.

For a moment our gaze held each other's. I wasn't intimidated or afraid anymore, but I was completely bewildered and still not sure what to do with this. I barely knew him, and my situation hadn't changed. I was not available in any way. Well, except in the way that led to flaming-hot fucks in five-star bathrooms. It was like we were animals or something. Very pampered animals, I supposed. I blinked down as warmth filled my cheeks and turned the water off.

We had to exit, and I wasn't sure what might be waiting on the other side. Neither of us had attempted to control the volume of our voices. Had someone alerted the management? I wouldn't even have heard if someone knocked during what just happened.

"Would you like me to go first?" His deep voice spoke to the fears in my mind.

Without answering, I reached forward and flipped the lock back, pulling the handle down and walking out casually. The passage was empty, and I exhaled with relief. No one was waiting outside, no hotel security, and the only persons I saw were hastening in our direction—but not to us, to the bar behind us.

I walked over to the water-fountain on the opposite wall. Just as I reached it, I heard the metallic door open, and I knew Derek was emerging. I stood and wiped my mouth, turning to face him. When my eyes hit his, my chest clenched. My type or not, he was gorgeous. The light blue shirt stretched across the top of his perfect chest made his eyes glow, and his dark, wavy locks were pushed back from his face. He caught my gaze with an expression of true appreciation, and my whole body warmed. What was I doing? For that matter, who was I? I had no answer.

"We should probably head back to the restaurant," I said as he stepped toward me. "Patrick and Elaine might wonder."

"I told them I'd be sure you got back to your room safely."

I nodded, exhaling a short laugh, thinking of Elaine's plans. "They might actually be glad we're gone."

He lifted my hand into the crook of his muscled arm.

"You need to eat. Would you let me buy you dinner?"

We were slowly approaching the place where we first met, and I still wasn't sure I had much of an appetite. "Let's see what they're serving at the bar."

Only a few steps and we were there, but the music reached us outside, loud and pulsing. It sounded like a party, and not at all what I was in the mood for.

Derek stopped, placing his large hand over mine holding his arm. "Maybe we can see what they'll bring us outside? Beside the fire pit?"

He turned and led us out the side door to lounge chairs and an arrangement that mirrored ours on the spa side of the resort.

"Will this do?" he said, holding out my hand and stepping around the wooden loveseat, over which an Indian-designed blanket was thrown.

"It's lovely," I said, stepping forward and sitting.

"You're lovely," he said softly. "I couldn't take my eyes off you when you walked in tonight. I think red is your color."

A feeling I would not acknowledge warmed my stomach. It was something I couldn't allow to develop for him, not now.

"Thank you," I said, and my mind filled with images of what prompted our last exchange of thanks. The sensations flooding my insides grew stronger.

"If no one comes out, I'll walk in and order whatever looks good," he said.

I nodded, and for several moments we only sat watching the orange flames dance over the coals. It was hypnotic and very relaxing. Derek was beside me on the love seat, and our sides were pressed together. After what felt like many long moments, but what was probably only five, he tugged on my waist. I glanced at him and a smile touched his lips. At that, I leaned against him, resting my head on his firm chest. His muscular arm went around my shoulder and down my side.

We were so familiar with each other's bodies. We knew exactly how to touch one another to provoke the strongest response. But how did we relate in a casual setting like this? With our clothes on?

"Where did you grow up?" I asked, watching the fire.

"South Louisiana," he said. I felt his fingers lifting clumps of my curls and holding them. "And you?"

"Atlanta," I said. "But only until I was nine. Then we moved to the coast, just outside Wilmington, North Carolina. That's where I met Elaine."

"You've known each other that long?" He was still playing with my hair, and I found it unexpectedly soothing. Even though we barely knew each other, I felt incredibly safe with him.

"She's the closest thing to a sister I have. She's always been there for me."

We were quiet again, and at last a waitress appeared. "Can I bring you a drink?" she asked.

"Yes," Derek's voice was full of authority. "A bottle of cava, two glasses, and two of your olive-salad sandwiches."

The young woman nodded, and hastened away.

"In south Louisiana, those are called muffulettas," I said, resting my head back against his chest.

"You've been to New Orleans?"

"No," I smiled, "but I read a lot."

His hand traced circles on my upper arm, and I could feel my eyelids drooping. Sitting here with him, under the desert sky with the temperature dropping, watching the fire in the pit and waiting on olive-salad sandwiches, I could almost pretend we were a couple. That I was a normal person on a holiday with my boyfriend, without a care in the world.

But I wasn't.

I stirred and started to move away, but his arm tightened over me. "What's wrong?"

"I really should head back to my room. It's late."

He released his hold on me, which was good because he was a thousand times stronger than I was. I couldn't have fought him if I tried, and for a moment, I considered that might be the reason I'd always avoided such muscular men. Not because they weren't attractive, because he was damn sexy.

"Just stay and have your dinner first," he said.

As if on cue, the young waitress appeared with a tray holding a dark green bottle, two clear silicone wine glasses, and two large sandwiches. She placed the entire load on the small table in front of us and handed it out.

"Shall I charge this to your room?" she asked.

"Two thirteen," he said.

I didn't want to remember the number, but it seemed the harder I tried to forget it, the more firmly it was imprinted on my brain.

"I thought hotels always skipped thirteen," I said. "Bad luck."

"I don't believe in luck."

A popping sound announced the opening of the cava, which the waitress poured into the glasses for each of us. I took mine and waited until she'd put the bottle in a small stoneware bucket and gone.

"Are we still celebrating?" I asked.

His dark eyes met mine, and for a moment we didn't speak, he only studied my face. I was starting to grow self-conscious when he broke the silence.

"Every day's a celebration, right? We're alive?"

I smiled and nodded, tapping my glass against his. He put his down on the table and picked up his huge sandwich.

"We could've split one," I said evaluating the size of mine. "Half would be plenty for me."

He smiled. "But not for me."

I gingerly took a bite and set the savory concoction back on the plate. The sharp cheese flavor filled my mouth, and I thought it was the perfect blend of tangy and salty.

"So you're a Marine?" I asked, watching him chew.

He nodded, swallowing. "Did my tour in Iraq during the first Gulf War."

"You must've been just a boy!"

"Eighteen," he said, lifting the glass and taking a sip of cava.

"And the special forces?"

"Did that for a while after, before I retired and went to the police academy."

I nodded. "How long were you a police officer?"

"I wasn't," he said with a smile.

"But…"

"I bypassed that and got my private investigator's license. In college I studied finance, and with the Internet taking off, I wanted to hunt down cyber-criminals. I worked in Law Enforcement Online a bit."

"What's that?" I studied his dark hair in the moonlight, imagining him in uniform, in the desert, fighting terrorists. It was an extremely attractive image.

"LEO is a branch of the FBI."

"So you're a special agent?"

He laughed. "No. I just worked there a little while."

"What do they do?"

"It's pretty complicated, and much of it's classified. How about we just leave it as is?"

"But you don't do it anymore?" I pressed. Then I wondered why I even cared so much. I didn't need to know all of this about him. We were just in this for a week. He could put himself in as much danger as he chose. I'd never see him again.

The thought made my stomach clench painfully.

He shook his head. "Now I'm freelance. I work with banks to hunt down cyber criminals. People who would steal customers' money or attempt to make fraudulent transactions. Hack into online bank accounts, phishers. Things like that."

I pressed my lips together and nodded. "Still a hero."

He shrugged. "I travel a lot. Do these conferences. I'm as much an educator as anything."

"And do you have a girl at each stop?" I froze. I didn't know where that question came from. "I'm sorry," I said quickly. "It's not really my business —"

"No." He cut me off, staring straight into my eyes. "I don't have a girl anywhere. Actually, I've never done anything like this before."

Suddenly we were both very quiet. I looked at the half-eaten sandwich on my plate and realized I was finished. I didn't want any more wine. I needed to get back to my room, to get my head straight. We were venturing into impossible territory now.

I stood quickly. "Thank you so much for dinner," I said, dusting my hands together.

Derek stood just as fast, towering over me in the night. "Please don't go," he said. "It's still early."

I shook my head. "It's late, and I'm tired. And... well... I think we both know it's for the best."

Just as I turned to leave, I felt his touch, light at my elbow. "See me tomorrow. Don't stay away. It's just for a few more days."

His words, the tone in his voice, caused a sharp pain in the center of my body. It was as if a sword were thrust into the space below my ribs, above my stomach. I glanced back at his blue eyes, bright and open. It was impossible to believe I could have any power over him at all, but it seemed in this one request, I did.

I nodded. "What would you like to do?"

He smiled and lowered his hand. "What's your last name?"

I shook my head. "My room is 323 in the spa tower. Call me that way."

The crease in his brow told me he didn't understand, but if he truly had access to all of our background information like Patrick had teased, I didn't want him knowing what my year had been like. I didn't want anyone knowing. Having not gone officially on record, I wasn't sure if he could find anything out, but I couldn't be too careful.

"Goodnight," I said leaning forward to kiss his cheek, cutting off any further discussion. Just as I was about to pull back, he caught the back of my neck and pulled my mouth to his for a better kiss.

I didn't resist, allowing his soft lips to part mine. I placed my palms on his strong shoulders, bracing myself as our tongues entwined. His kiss turned hungry, and my mouth matched his pace. I wanted him to lift me again. I craved the connection of our bodies as much as he did. Heat flared between my legs, but I resisted, stepping back, inhaling deeply, eyes still closed.

"Goodnight," I said, this time in a shaky whisper.

My eyes blinked open and only briefly caught his before I turned and walked away, not giving him a chance to respond.

CHAPTER 5 – LITTLE BOXES

Our room was dim and empty when I arrived. The turn-down service had left organic dark chocolates on our pillows and soft track lighting ran around the walls behind the headboards. Beach sounds were coming from the little music station between the two beds, and the air smelled faintly of the signature cactus flower perfume. Everything was designed to cultivate a relaxed, spa vibe. I actually liked it.

Elaine was still with Patrick, I supposed. I went to the bathroom and flicked on the soft yellow lights, and for a moment, I was stunned by my reflection. My cheeks did seem rosier, and although the faint lines were still visible at the corners of my eyes, even my eyes were different. The smallest hint of that old brightness was fighting to return. Was it all the spa pampering? The easy, schedule-less days of sleeping in and then relaxing by the pool, allowing the nonstop tension to drain from my body?

Or was it him?

I shook my head and tied my long dark curls back so I could wash my face. Once I was finished and had smoothed a thin line of moisturizer under my eyes and across my lips, I turned and walked back to the large, queen-sized bed where I slept. My phone lay discarded at the foot. I hadn't even thought about taking it with me. I didn't want to check emails or texts. I was in a bubble, and everyone had been informed I would be unavailable for the week. I had auto-respond messages set up everywhere.

But still he called.

Sloan's picture and number sat there staring at me like the cat that always came back. Tonight I didn't listen to his message. I didn't want to hear his lectures. I tossed the phone on the small sofa in our room and slipped between the cool, crisp sheets. I considered deleting his contact information, getting a new phone, a new number. But no. I needed to know where he was. At least for now.

Pushing aside those dark thoughts, I inhaled Derek's warm, woodsy scent again in my hair. A little smile teased at the corner of my lips when I thought of how wild our encounters were. I slid my dark locks across my face, closing my eyes and imagining his strong arms around my waist, remembering him pushing me against the wall. The feel of that huge man trembling in my arms when he came. The sound of his groans.

Lying in the dark alone, I did the one thing that would drive my mother crazy. I compartmentalized it all. With my eyes closed, I imagined taking Sloan and putting him alone in his own, cold plastic box. I slammed the lid and shoved it on a back shelf in my mind. Then I gathered all the events of the last year as if scooping up scattered blocks and dumped them in another box, which I shoved under Sloan's.

Stretching out in my bed, I took a new box. I imagined lining it with satin and flower petals. I took little pillows and made a soft bed. That's where I put Derek and his memories. I pictured myself small, climbing into the box with him. He was lying back on the cushions in his grey slacks. The button-down he wore was open, and I could see every line on his sculpted torso. That little smile was on his lips as he watched me approach. I ran my fingers along the lines of his stomach, gazing into his eyes that darkened as I touched him.

His kiss, the same one he gave me beside the fire pit, was gentle but hungry. Our pace grew faster as we kissed each other again and again, tongues entwining, heat growing between my legs, until he pulled me under him. My breathing was fast, my whole body tense with anticipation, so wet, so ready for his awesome fullness. I felt his tip pressing into me, filling me, as a thought drifted through my mind. *We'd never done it in a bed...*

* * *

Scuffing sounds and the loud noise of someone trying to be quiet woke me. I looked at the clock. It wasn't even eight yet. Elaine was hurrying around the room, filling a bag with her bathing suit, a towel,

"What are you doing?" I asked, my voice thick with sleep.

"Oh," she exclaimed. "I'm sorry! I didn't mean to wake you."

I sat up slowly, rubbing my eyes. Looking around, I almost expected to see Derek in bed with me. I'd drifted to sleep in our box, wrapped in his huge, protective arms.

"Did you spend the night with Patrick?" I asked.

A giggle was followed quickly by a throat clearing. "Yes," she said, unable to hide her beaming face. "Oh my god."

My lips pressed into a smile. "Good?"

"Holy fuck," she flopped across the foot of my bed. "I think I came five times last night."

I grinned, smoothing her now-messy blonde hair. "Is it possible to meet your soul mate in one day?" she asked, looking up at me.

"No idea," I said, not wanting to think about questions like that. It made my stomach hurt. "I'm not sure I believe in soul mates. But you like him? Sounds like poor Brian is definitely toast."

"Don't even say the B-word. Patrick is the hottest thing. And that body." She did a little shiver. "First we just talked all hours. Oh! You never came back. Did Derek find you? He said not to worry, and I figured since he's practically a cop and a Marine..."

I bit my lip, still not sure how much I wanted to tell her about Derek's and my... relationship? Agreement? I didn't have a clue what to call it. I'd never had a fuck buddy before. Were we even buddies? We never saw each other outside of patios, bars, and family restrooms.

"We... bumped into each other," I said. Then I suppressed a grin at how that "bump" went. And how hot and noisy it was.

"Did you get any dinner?"

"I did, but tell me about you and Patrick."

"Mmm," she smiled again. "Okay, like I said, first we talked all hours, really got to know each other. Then we went down to the pool. It was completely dark, so we sneaked in—"

"You went skinny dipping?"

She giggled. "Have you ever had sex in a pool? It is *amazing*. Everything's all wet, and the water was the exact right temperature."

"I hope you used protection." I mentally wondered at how many public decency laws these former cops of ours broke.

"Of course!" Elaine jumped up and went back to filling her bag. "He's going to blow off the conference today, and we're spending it together. When I told him this was my first trip to Arizona, he had all these places I just *have* to see."

"Sounds like fun," I sighed, rolling onto my side.

Then her expression changed. "I'm sorry!" she cried. "I'm the worst friend ever! I need to stay with you and do our treatments. Our mental health regimen."

I sat up and shook my head. "No way! Get out of here! I'm the one who needs a mental health regimen. You can catch up with me tonight."

She bounced over and kissed my cheek. "Thanks," she cooed. "I'll make it up to you. Promise."

* * *

Once Elaine was gone, I lay back in the bed again, remembering my little box with Derek and wanting to climb back inside and wrap myself in his arms. Last night he'd entered me from behind, kissing my neck, his scruffy beard teasing the sensitive places around my shoulders.

His large fingers massaged my clit until I came so hard…

I blinked at the ceiling a few times acknowledging it was all a fantasy—at least that version of us together was. It had been *my* small fingers doing the massaging, and nothing teased the sensitive areas of my shoulders, although the idea of that still made me shiver.

I threw back the covers and got up, shaking the crazy out of my brain. Everything in my life had been upended, and now I was thousands of miles from home, having sex with a practical stranger and inventing an entire fantasy-life around him. Maybe I did need some time on Mom's couch.

As if on cue, my phone flashed her photograph, silently vibrating in the chair where I'd tossed it last night. I'd been avoiding her calls, not wanting to tell her what was happening. But I couldn't hide forever.

I slid my finger across the face. "Hi, Mom."

"Melissa, where are you?" Her stern voice was tinged with worry. I was almost sure I knew why.

"I'm with Elaine, Mom, why?"

She exhaled into the receiver. "You're at the beach? Why didn't you tell me you were headed this way?"

I bit my lip, choosing my words, still fishing for why she might be calling. "What's got you so worked up?"

"Sloan called this morning looking for you, and I didn't know what to tell him."

My chest clenched. *Bingo.* "I'm just taking a mental health break. You're a big advocate of those, right?"

"Do you need to make an appointment? Maybe with Robin? I know she could work you in if you're in town."

Talking to Mom's partner was actually a great idea. Dr. Taylor was compassionate and didn't take sides.

Although everyone had already taken sides in my case it seemed.

"I'm actually not in town, Mom. I'm in the desert."

"What? Where?"

"This spa resort... somewhere. It's really nice."

She didn't answer, and I could tell she wasn't happy with my evasiveness.

"Look, I'm really trying to get away from everything for a few days, get my head together," I said. "I'm with Elaine, so I'm fine. Let's just leave it at that."

She finally spoke slowly. "I don't like it. What if something happened? I wouldn't even know how to find you."

"You just did," I sighed. "Please. Trust me?"

I heard her matching my exhale. "When will you be back?"

"We're only here a week. I'll be in Baltimore on Monday."

"Call me when you get there."

I agreed and hung up, but the image of me back in Maryland was almost too painful to conjure. Every time I tried, all I could see was me walking, shoulders stooped, as if an invisible weight were strapped to them, dragging me down, lower and lower. This trip had been an escape I needed more than even I'd realized. Elaine had seen something I couldn't see. I was desperate, and it was only getting worse the longer I stayed there.

Being here was like taking a deep breath of fresh air, like standing up straight for the first time in a year. Now I wasn't sure if I'd be able to return to that old life, even for a day.

I rubbed my forehead and went into the bathroom. But I had to go back, at least to get my things, close up my office... I'd worry about those details when the time came. As it was, I still had three more days, and if I were counting time with Derek, they would be pretty incredible.

I lifted the red bikini off the bathroom hook and swept my hair into a high ponytail. If Elaine was gone all day, I was spending it at the pool.

CHAPTER 6 – ALL SORTS OF OPTIONS

After an entire morning in the desert sun, I was now under the umbrella, sipping a wine spritzer, my plate of raw-food "lunch" devoured. Elaine's review boards were entirely right about everything at the Cactus Flower Spa. The pool boys were sexy, the massages were divine, and the raw food menu was for the birds. Literally. I was dying for a luscious steak dinner with all the trimmings.

Holding my magazine, I noticed a change in the light and glanced up expecting another visit by my server. I didn't expect to see Derek, looking fantastic in navy swim shorts and a maroon tee, holding a spa-issued towel. His blue eyes were hidden behind aviator sunglasses, but his dark hair moved easily in the dry breeze. A smile of approval was on his lips, and my entire body lit up like a firecracker.

"Red is definitely your color," he said in that low voice that made me wish for the nearest family bathroom.

"Hello," I said, pushing myself into a sitting position on the lounger. My cover-up was on my shoulders, but it was open, revealing the swimsuit he obviously admired. "Finished for the day?"

"Maybe," he said, sitting on the chair next to mine. "I was craving a dip in the pool. Or something."

I smiled, almost, but not quite sure of his meaning. "I'm surprised they let you in the way they guard this place. Did you bribe one of the clinicians?"

"Yes," he said, pulling off his shirt. "A cool fifty, and the doors flew open."

The sight of his perfect chest and lined stomach caught my breath. Less than twenty-four hours ago, I'd been wrapped around him, and I was growing slick at the memory. I blinked down to the shimmering pool water, my whole body flushed.

"How did you find me?" I managed to say.

"I'm a detective, after all."

I returned his grin at that. "Oh, really?"

He chuckled. "Last night you told me your room number. I called and they said you were here."

I wasn't pleased with them giving out my location to unknown gentlemen callers, but in this case, I'd let it slide. My eyes drifted to the round tattoo near his shoulder. It was an anchor design blended with a skull over an *SF*.

"And that's for…?"

He seemed confused then glanced down. "Oh. Marines." He shook his head. "Rite of passage, I guess."

"It's cool. Unique."

"I really enjoyed dinner on the patio last night," he continued, leaning back. "When Patrick said he was blowing off the day, I considered doing the same."

I slanted my eyes at him, confident enough to flirt. "Why didn't you?"

"Had a workshop at ten. But it was hard to concentrate."

One of the slim, tanned pool boys who just moments ago I'd conceded was "sexy" walked up. Now he looked like a child to me. "Drink, sir?"

Derek glanced over at the table beside me. "Two of whatever the lady's having."

The boy nodded and quickly left.

"It's just a wine spritzer, I should warn you."

That grin was back on his lips, making me want to kiss them. "What's with you and ordering drinks?"

I bit my lip unsure of how much to reveal. Then I shrugged. "It's been a while since I've done it for myself."

His blue eyes flickered to my face behind his glasses. I could tell his interest was piqued, and he wanted me to say more. "Sounds like a story."

I lifted the glass from the table beside me and finished the rest of my drink just as the server returned with two new ones.

"Maybe I'll tell it to you sometime." I was relaxed from the alcohol, and wanting to stay in this place of bliss with him. "But not now. It's too depressing."

He nodded. Then he sat up. "I'm taking a dip. It's warmer than I expected."

I watched as he stood and walked to the pool. He was literally perfect, and I noticed many eyes following him into the water. He submerged beneath the crystal blue surface and shot to the other side of the long pool.

Up until now, he'd been the initiator of all our encounters. Elaine was gone for the day, our room was empty. Would I invite him up? Did I want to get that close? As I pondered the question, he surfaced on the other side of the pool. Wiping his eyes he turned, then went under and shot back in my direction. In moments, he was back, surfacing in front of me, and when our blue eyes met, a loud *Yes!* echoed in my head.

Standing, I let my cover-up slide off my shoulders, and I tossed it on the lounge chair. My hair was still in a high ponytail, and as I walked to meet him in the pool, his eyes tracked my progress. He leaned back against the side, stretching his arms out, and his focused attention set my pulse humming under my skin. With every step, desire throbbed stronger in my core, and by the time I lowered myself into the pool, it was all I could do to keep my hands to myself. I pictured drifting one under the water to his waist, running my fingers down the front of his swim trunks, coaxing him to an erection. His face said it wouldn't take much. But I kept my expression neutral.

"The water's nice," I said, leaning against the wall beside him.

He nodded. "Refreshing."

"This morning I was thinking how little we know about each other."

His eyes were still on me, traveling from my face to my hair then back to my mouth, where they lingered. My lips tingled for his touch.

"What do you want to know?" His tone had become low and sexy.

"I don't know," I said, trying to think of neutral things we could share. Questions that wouldn't lead to subjects I didn't want to discuss.

"What's your favorite color?"

"Red," he answered quickly.

I smiled, and my cheeks warmed. "Seriously."

He leaned forward, returning my smile as he lowered his arms into the water. "I've never really had a favorite color until now."

I turned and bent my elbows on the side, resting them on the mosaic tiles leading into the pool. We were so close, my upper arm touched his shoulder. It was electric.

"Okay," I said slowly, thinking. "What was your favorite game as a boy?"

"Football."

A little laugh escaped my lips, and I lay my cheek on my forearms. "You're not giving me anything memorable."

His hand drifted under the water to my side, where he lightly ran the back of his fingers down my skin from my ribs to my hip. My eyes closed as desire flooded into my lower abdomen, and I fought a moan.

"I'll tell you something memorable," he said in that sensual voice. "But I'd rather do it in private."

My eyes opened slowly, and I wondered if he could read my thoughts. He turned and pushed against the tiles, his muscles flexing as he rose out of the water. Little droplets ran down his torso, and an image of me licking them off almost made me burst into flames. I quickly followed him out and back to our things on the lounge chairs. Our wine still sat on the small table between them.

"Should we take our drinks upstairs?" I said.

"I was waiting for you to ask."

* * *

Being in my bed allowed for all sorts of options. We'd already recreated my fantasy from the little box, only in reality, he held me on his lap, both of us in a sitting position as he filled me with his huge cock from behind. My back was pressed against his firm chest, and with one hand, he squeezed my breast while the other massaged my rigid clit. I couldn't stop the little moans that drove him wild. I barely even knew I was making them as his mouth covered my neck with burning kisses, his beard scratching the back of my shoulders. All I knew was him full inside me, pushing all the way in, harder as I rose on my knees and then dropped, increasing the depth of his thrusts.

"Fuck," he groaned, the hand that was holding my breast now moved to my stomach, pulling me harder against him. Our thighs crashed as I moved on him, and the sensation of his rock-hard dick hitting my G-spot while his expert fingers massaged my clit conjured images I'd seen of women coming like men, wet and everywhere. Three more hard thrusts, and I was flying to the moon.

I dropped my head back and came so hard, my whole body shook. He kept pushing, and I gripped his hands, squirming and moaning, desperate for him to keep going, but unsure if I could take any more of this intense pleasure.

"Ooh, god," I wailed, and we both slid forward onto the bed. He was still inside me gently thrusting, and I rubbed my thighs together, shaking but easing down from the rocket high I'd just hit, savoring the feel of his huge cock massaging my return.

I lay on my stomach, Derek propped behind me, watching me, his pace slowing. We were both breathing so hard, I could feel his warm breath against my back.

As much as I hated losing our connection, I slipped off him and turned, resting my cheek on his chest and wrapping my arms around his waist. His strong arms went around me, holding me securely several long moments as my body calmed. Inhaling him deeply, I placed a small kiss against his skin.

"Did you finish?" I whispered.

He chuckled. "If I hadn't been wearing a condom, it might've shot out your ears I came so hard."

My nose wrinkled, but I had to laugh. "That's a lovely image."

"You drive me crazy." His hands went to my shoulders, and he eased up to look into my eyes. "I don't know what to do with you. With this."

I blinked down, not wanting to start this conversation with him. He wouldn't like the way it ended. I didn't like the way it ended in my mind.

"You seem to have a pretty good idea what to do with me," I tried deflecting.

I pulled away from his gaze, resting my cheek against his chest once more. His fingers traced lines down my back, and I closed my eyes, loving this moment, wanting to permanently brand it on my memory so I'd never forget it. Never forget him.

"That night you didn't meet me, I was pretty frustrated," he said. "All day I'd caught your scent on my hair, my beard... then I showered before going to the bar, and you were gone."

I chewed my lip thinking how I'd done the same — lifted my dark curls to smell his warm woodsy scent that was now all around me, filling my bed.

"I was desperate to see you one more time just to get that luscious scent on me again," he finished.

I lifted my head, teasing. "Are you saying you haven't showered in two days?"

He caught my cheeks and pulled my lips to his, covering my mouth in a gentle kiss. My lips parted and the tips of our tongues touched lightly, setting off a little spark below my waist.

"I'm just giving you a peek at what you're doing to me," he said, his voice low.

I slid down, resting my cheek on his firm pectorals, tracing the lines with my fingers. We were quiet a moment, then I thought of us at the pool, our unfinished conversation. "You were going to tell me something memorable," I said.

His hand returned to my back where he lightly touched my skin. "Yes," he murmured, and my head rose with his inhale. "What do you want to know?"

Everything, my stubborn mind answered. Instead, I said, "You were telling me about when you were a boy. Your favorite game. Start there."

He was quiet, thoughtful. "My dad was in the military. A few times when I was pretty young, he was sent on missions where I knew he might not come back."

He paused, but my interest was piqued. "How did you know?" I asked.

"I could tell by the way my mom cried when he left." His hand continued stroking my back. "It scared me so bad I couldn't sleep at night."

In my mind, I pictured a kid-sized version of him, dark hair, blue eyes, lying alone in the dark. Afraid. It was an image I could relate to well, and instinctively, my arm went around his waist.

"What did you do?" I said.

His tone remained calm, comforting. "I made up a game. I thought about my favorite thing to do with my dad. And I decided as soon as he got back, we'd do that together."

"What was it?"

He inhaled deeply. "Different things. Sometimes it was as simple as throwing a football together. But focusing on us doing it, having fun, smiling, helped me know I'd survive the pain of waiting."

My eyes were damp. "It's a very sophisticated approach for a little kid."

I felt him shrug. "It didn't solve the problem. It just gave it an end point."

I thought about what he was saying, and I thought about my situation. "But what if it feels like the pain will never go away?"

His hand stilled on my back. "It will. Eventually. Sometimes you're not even aware it's gone and then something happens, something unexpected, and you realize it's no longer there."

I lifted off him, sliding my fingers under my lower lashes before propping my head on my hand. He wrapped a dark curl around his finger as his gaze traveled from my lips to my eyes. I wanted to know what he meant, if he had experience with pain like that, like mine, but we were venturing far too close to off-limits topics. Instead I changed directions.

"So you followed in your dad's footsteps and joined the military," I said, looking back at his beautiful blues. "You were so young. What was it like in Iraq?"

His lips tightened. "Lonely. Scary at times."

"Did you use your game?"

A small smile touched his lips. "Sometimes."

"Did it work?"

His eyes moved away from mine, and he didn't answer.

Then it struck me—he might have things he didn't want to share as well.

"I'm sorry," I said. "We're probably breaking the rules of a one-week stand."

"Probably," he said, but his tone was different. "I wouldn't know."

We'd gone too far, and it was my fault. I had wanted to ask questions. I wanted to know everything about him. But I'd forgotten I couldn't. No matter how my heart craved knowing him, what we were doing couldn't last beyond this week. When I left this place, I returned to everything I was pretending didn't exist, and that was no place for him.

The thought pressed on my mind, threatening to spoil our private escape. So I lowered my hand and moved up to kiss him, to take us back to what we were able to share. My hands cupped his cheeks, and his fingers that had been tracing lines on my skin began massaging, moving lower. I rolled onto my back, tugging his shoulders as I did. He readily complied, rising above me, deepening our kiss.

My hands moved from his shoulders, down his arms, finding his hard stomach. His lips pressed mine apart as his tongue swept inside to curl around mine. My legs opened automatically, allowing him between them, and in a breath, he pushed inside me, hard and full. We hadn't done much foreplay, and we'd only just come down from our last shattering climax. But it didn't matter. I was already wet. The little we had shared deepened my desire for him, and the fullness of him pushing into me, combined with his mouth covering mine, moving to my jaw, lightly nibbling on my neck, sent heat shimmering down my legs.

My insides bonded to him, melted into him, wrapped around him, holding him to me. But I couldn't name what I was feeling.

Never in my life had I dreamed I would enjoy being with someone like him so much, and now I couldn't imagine having anyone else in my bed. He was enormous over me — I was only five four, almost a whole foot shorter and just at 120 pounds — and I knew I'd never be satisfied with anything less again.

"You're so quiet," he whispered against my ear before kissing it, still rocking into me slowly.

I was holding him, loving the feel of his fullness sliding in and out of me. He kissed my neck again, and I wrapped my arms tighter over his shoulders. I never wanted to let him go.

"Mmm," I breathed. "It's even good slow."

His hands moved to my buttocks and together we rolled over so that I was on top. But I stayed with my torso pressed against his, kissing his mouth, kissing a trail down his neck to his chest.

A low groan vibrated through his upper body, and I sped up my rocking. Instantly, the friction triggered my climb, and I increased the pace. I sat up fully then, bucking my hips against his pelvis as he watched me. My dark curls spilling all around me.

"Fuck, Mel," he gasped. "You're so hot. I'm fucking about to come again."

He gripped my butt, easily lifting me up and down and he seemed to grow larger. I was moaning now as the pressure built in my legs, tightened through my lower abdomen.

"Fuck," he murmured again, increasing the speed as he lifted me, slamming me back down against his hips. "I can't hold it."

I felt him shoot off and instantly my orgasm exploded through my legs. He was still lifting me up and down, and I collapsed forward, pulsing in his arms. He gently stopped lifting me and held me as we rolled back to him on top, still inside me.

"I'm sorry," he breathed, lifting up and fixing his blue eyes on mine. "I wasn't expecting that. I didn't have a chance to prepare."

For a moment, I didn't want to move. The sensations humming under my skin were so strong, so sensual. My eyes slowly opened, and I studied his beautiful face, tracing a finger over his dark brow, thinking how fantastically our bodies worked together. I had a hard time wrapping my mind around it.

"It's okay," I whispered. "I'm still on the pill."

The dark brows I'd just caressed drew together. "Sounds like I had a lucky slip."

A tiny laugh slipped out with my exhale. He had no idea. "You could say that."

"When I told you that first night I was clean, I was being honest," he said, the powerful hands that were so strong to lift me—and probably anything else—gently traveled up my body, smoothing back my hair. "It's been a while since I've been with anyone, and last time I checked, I was all clear."

I nodded. "I've never done anything like this before," I whispered. "But I've had a reason to keep up with things. You're safe with me."

He lowered his face to kiss me gently and right then it was inescapable. The seemingly endless kiss he pressed, soft lips lingering against mine, tongue lightly touching my tongue, sealed it for me. He was everything I wanted. He *was* safe with me, I felt safe with him, and I wanted him to hold me forever so badly.

But in that simple acknowledgment, my heart sank in my chest. This blissful paradise we were sharing, our strange arrangement, was drowned by my dismal reality. I was not one he could hold.

CHAPTER 7 – WHAT I'D GIVE YOU

Elaine and Patrick met us for dinner in the hotel restaurant. They were beaming like blissed-out honeymooners and seemed unable to stop touching each other in little ways, laughing easily and holding hands. I figured they'd spent the day doing at least a little of what Derek and I'd shared, and I wished I was free to look at him that way, to share my passion for him so overtly.

Everything in me was falling in love with Derek, but that didn't change a single thing about my situation. About my unavailability. Add to that, he hadn't said anything to indicate he wanted more than our original week. It felt like he might want more, every time we were together I was sure his feelings were growing as intensely as mine, but he hadn't said anything to confirm it.

Following our last round this afternoon, I'd fallen asleep in his arms and vaguely remembered waking as he slid from my side, lightly kissing my head and whispering that he'd see me at dinner. I'd continued sleeping another hour before I'd risen to shower.

Tonight, I wore a short, black dress with thin spaghetti straps. A sterling silver cuff bracelet was on my wrist and large silver hoop earrings were the extent of my accessorizing. As always, Derek smiled, clearly pleased with my appearance. The three were already sharing a bottle of wine when I joined them, Derek stood to help me in my chair.

"You look beautiful," he said softly, his breath whispering over my shoulder, causing a shiver to tingle through me.

Neither Elaine nor Patrick even noticed, and I was pretty sure they were oblivious to the connection between their dinner mates. All they were focused on was the growing connection between the two of them.

Derek poured me a glass of wine, and I took it with a little nod of thanks. Patrick broke his nonstop gazing at my best friend to greet me.

"So it seems you had a fun day?" I said, teasing.

Elaine flushed. "You could say that."

I tried for a neutral subject, something we could all discuss, and since Patrick had told us so much about their work last night, it seemed a safe option. "You never told me where you two are based, where your office is located," I said.

Patrick smiled, sipping his wine. "Princeton."

"New Jersey?" I asked, slightly stunned. Princeton was an easy two-hour drive from my office in Baltimore, as I knew well. The accompanying thoughts his words conjured made my stomach burn.

"Derek teaches a few classes at the university."

"You do?" Elaine asked.

"We're hardly there," Derek added quickly, and for a moment, he almost seemed annoyed at Patrick's answer.

"I had a client at Princeton once," I said, not sure how those words managed to creep out. Elaine's eyes cut to mine.

"Really?" Patrick said. "Who was it?"

"Sloan Reynolds." Saying his name left a foul taste in my mouth, and I wished I'd never brought it up. I wanted off this train of thought. "I did some work for his family, actually."

The conversation momentarily stalled as Patrick seemed to think. "Don't know him," he finally said. "Sorry."

"It was several years ago." I finished that topic, taking a sip of my wine to cleanse my palate.

Patrick looked down then held his wine glass aloft, turning back to Elaine. "To unexpected surprises."

My friend beamed at that. "Isn't it the truth?"

They clinked glasses and Patrick covered Elaine's hand with his again, smiling.

I looked back at Derek, giving him a tight smile. "It's so bright in here."

His eyes were warm now, focused on me. "The fire pit is a much nicer setting, I think."

"And you're in Wilmington," Patrick said to Elaine.

"Yep," my friend replied. "Been there all my life. It's where Melissa and I met."

Derek glanced at me. "But you're not there now."

"No," I said softly, wondering when I'd been so unguarded to tell him that. My home location was definitely a one-week stand rules violation.

"She's hours away in Baltimore," Elaine complained.

"It's only six hours. Don't exaggerate." Now I wished I'd thought up a different topic of conversation. I wanted this exploration into my personal life to end. "So tell me about your day. What all did you do?"

That did it. Instantly she was off describing their hike up Camelback Mountain. They'd found a secret cleft in the rocks, she continued, and from the way my friend grinned at that detail, it seemed they'd done more than hike while there. Patrick smiled and squeezed her hand, a little spark in his eye. Our waiter took our orders, and I selected the steak I'd been craving earlier. Derek followed suit.

"At least your food orders are better than your drinks," he teased.

I smiled. "I never stopped choosing my own food."

"Shall I pick a wine to go with it?"

"Please do," I said, wishing I could reach out and touch his hand the way our dinner companions kept doing. His eyes flickered to mine, and it seemed he might be thinking the same thing.

Elaine continued detailing their day, a tour of Taliesin West, a visit to one of the nearby ghost towns. I was amazed they'd been able to fit it all in.

"Tomorrow I was thinking we'd drive to Sedona," Patrick said, looking at Derek.

Derek waved his hand. "Do what you want. We're pretty much finished as far as the conference goes."

His words made my heart sink, knowing the end was so near. I lifted my glass and took a long sip of the pinot noir he'd ordered—perfect for the petite filet I was having. I felt him studying my reaction, and I wondered how he felt about the end of this week. Did it sadden him as much as it did me?

"We're pretty much done here," he said, rising. "I'll ask the host to put it on my bill if you'd like to take a walk outside with me?"

Elaine's eyes flew to mine, and she gave me an encouraging smile.

"Sure," I said, standing.

"I think you can take your glass if you'd like to finish it," Derek said, holding my chair.

"That's okay," I said. "I've had enough."

Patrick and Elaine stayed behind, and she smiled in a way that I knew meant she was dying to give me two thumbs up. If she only knew how behind she was. I just shook my head and took Derek's arm, allowing him to escort me from the large dining area.

It was another beautiful twilight, the sun slowly setting, turning the desert sky a myriad of dusky autumnal shades. I couldn't stop my mind from counting the time we had left—only two nights. We'd fly out early Sunday, and I'd return to my situation in Maryland.

We strolled along the path lining the resort's large golf course. I had so many things I wished I could say, and none that I could truly act upon. I wanted to exchange contact information, make plans to follow up when we got home, to be together, to hold onto him...

Derek wasn't speaking either. He seemed a million miles away, and I wondered if his thoughts were following a similar course as mine. As always, he was incredibly handsome in grey, tailored slacks and a navy, short-sleeved sweater. It was thin and hugged the lines of his torso.

"Patrick and Elaine seem to be enjoying the trip," I finally said, holding his arm as we walked.

"Hm," Derek nodded, but he didn't say more.

"Is anything wrong?" I asked, not sure if I wanted to know his answer. If something was wrong, and it was anything like I suspected, I wouldn't be able to ease his mind.

His forehead creased, and he looked out at the horizon, speaking quietly. "This afternoon, being with you… It wasn't what I expected."

"It wasn't?" My chest sank. To me this afternoon had set the bar on intensity so high, I was pretty sure I'd never top it. Hearing he might've thought less of it almost killed me.

He exhaled then gave me a sad little smile. "It was intense." We took a few more steps, and he added just above a whisper. "Too fucking intense."

My breath returned, and I gently squeezed his arm. "I've made some pretty lasting memories with you this week."

He stopped then and faced me. "Patrick's got a big mouth. He's said things about me I thought were best left off the record."

I looked down, not wanting to meet his eyes, not wanting him to see the tears forming in mine. "Elaine, too."

"In my line of work, when people don't want you to know their story, they usually have a damn good reason."

I wasn't sure if he was talking about himself or me, but I had to agree. "You're right."

"And pursuing that story only leaves everyone, well, pretty damaged." His voice wasn't angry, but it had a definite tone. I just couldn't tell what he was getting at. Was he saying he understood my need for privacy? Was he trying to tell me his? Or worse, was he trying to cut the week short? Had it gotten too intense for him?

The last thought sliced painfully through my heart. "Sometimes, the damage is already done."

"Listen to me," he put his hands on my cheeks and tilted my face up to look at his. When he saw my eyes glistening, his expression changed. His eyes closed and he lowered his forehead to mine, exhaling the words. "What have I done?"

My hands clasped over my aching heart. "What have you done?" I managed to say.

He'd fucking made me fall in love with him is what he'd done, and now I'd return to Baltimore worse off than when I got here. But I couldn't say that out loud. It wasn't his fault I'd lost control. He'd said one week. I was the one who'd ended up wanting everything I couldn't have.

He lifted his head and then kissed me, softly at first. His lips held mine a moment before the softness turned less gentle. His mouth moved, opening mine and finding my tongue. Heat flared through me as they touched, and his hands moved to my butt, lifting me against him. Easily my legs went around his waist, my arms around his neck. I was kissing him back in spite of the pain.

How could I waste time on self-preservation when our time together was so short? He broke our kiss, dropping his forehead to my cheek. His hands were securely holding my rear, and I moved my hands to his face, making him look up at me again. His brow was creased and his blue eyes were so earnest, yet so full of all the things he wouldn't tell me. How could I be angry when there were so many things I wouldn't tell him?

"If things were different," I said. "I'd tell you I love you right now."

His forehead relaxed, and his eyes closed. The smallest hint of a smile tried to form on his lips, but I wouldn't let myself see it. Instead I leaned forward and kissed him hard on the mouth. He kissed me back with an equal amount of passion, then I pushed against his chest, lowering my legs. He released me, brows pulled together again not understanding. I didn't stay to explain.

I turned and walked fast, not looking back. A few more steps and I was jogging across the grassy area that separated the patio from the spa hotel. He didn't follow me. He let me go back to my room, where I collapsed into the bed, tears rolling from my eyes.

* * *

Elaine didn't come back to the room that night, and when I awoke the next morning, a note had been slipped under the door.

Please call the front desk. A parcel has been left for you.

Curiously, I picked up the in-house phone and pressed 0. Alerting the hostess I was awake, she said she'd send the parcel right up, and I went to retrieve one of the thick robes that hung in the bathroom. I paused, checking my reflection. My eyes were only a little puffy from crying. I picked up a washcloth and wet it with cold water, holding it gently to them.

All night I'd dreamed of him. We didn't stay in the little box in my mind, we jumped out of it and ran free and clear all over my life. Derek carried me back to Wilmington, and we made love on the beach in my old hometown. We ran hand in hand through all of my favorite places from my memory, and everywhere he fit in as perfectly as if he was always meant to be there. It broke my heart. My dreams could be so cruel.

Just then the tapping started on my door. I jumped out of bed and ran across the room. The girl handed me a small package, and I handed her a tip. Then I closed the door and went back to the bed, ripping off the paper and pulling out a black velvet box.

For a moment, I hesitated. Then I carefully pulled the top open. Inside was a delicate gold chain on which a floating heart hung. A small note dropped out, and I opened it.

What I would give you. If you hadn't already stolen it. – D.A.

My lips pressed together as my eyes misted. Gently pulling the chain from the box, I fastened the necklace around my neck. The tag indicated it was 24 karat gold. It would never tarnish. I could leave it on forever if I chose. In the mirror in my room, I saw the delicate charm sat just at the base of my throat, in the little hollow between my collar bones where he'd often kissed me. I touched it gently.

He'd survive without his heart. He had mine to use in its place.

CHAPTER 8 – SOMETHING TRULY MAJOR

Elaine called to say she and Patrick were driving to Sedona as planned and wouldn't be back until late. I assured her I would be fine in her absence.

"Did you make any progress with Derek," she asked eagerly. "The man is sex on two legs, don't you think?"

Yes. "What are you saying?" I replied. "Aren't your eyes only for Patrick?"

"Of course! Patrick is amazing, and I'm not interested in trading at all. But I'm also not blind."

"Derek is very sexy."

"Very alpha," she said in a tone like she was reading my mind. "And ex-military. I know you tend to shy away from those."

I almost wished that were true. "He is a lot of man, but at the same time, he can be tender."

Her voice rose in excitement. "So you did get to know him better? Oh, Mel, if you got laid on this trip by that hunk of—"

"Hey," I cut her off. "Have fun today and be safe."

"You, too," she said. "Please do everything I would do."

I laughed, fingering the little heart floating at my neck as I hung up the phone. "Okay."

When I'd run off last night, leaving him at the fire pit, I'd also left without a plan for us meeting today. At the same time, when I reflected on our conversation up to that point, I wasn't sure if the door was still open to us meeting today.

Yes, I'd kissed him and told him I wished I could say I loved him. And he'd sent me this lovely gift, but the words we'd said before that...

Was it best to leave these tokens as our last goodbye?

Everything in me screamed *No!* If he was within steps of me, I had to try and find him. I considered going to Room 213 and pounding on his door, but I hesitated. If I did that, I'd be sending a message I couldn't live up to. I'd be saying I was his, and I couldn't say that.

I lay across my bed, again touching the floating heart on my neck. My eyes warmed. But I wanted to see him so badly. What could I do? As if on cue, my room telephone rang, and I snatched it up without hesitation.

"Good morning," his low voice touched me through the wires.

"Good morning," I replied softly. "I was just thinking about you. And you called."

"Did you get my gift?"

"I love it so much." My voice was tight with longing for what we couldn't have.

"I wasn't sure if you'd want to see me—"

"I do!" I sat straight up, clutching the receiver against my face as if it were his. "When? Where?"

He breathed a laugh. "Want to meet at the pool again?"

"Why don't we meet at the main hotel pool? Then you can save the fifty."

"It doesn't matter," he said. "I'd spend it again gladly."

"Give me thirty minutes," I said, throwing the covers back.

"I'll be there in five."

* * *

Walking out to the main pool, a dry breeze blew across the desert easing the heat beating against my face. The thin cover-up I'd slid over my shoulders billowed out behind me, and my red bikini glinted beneath it. The pool was enormous, and it seemed most of the conferees had decided to blow off their last day. I wasn't sure I'd find him, and for the first time, I regretted not having my mobile phone. Although, he didn't have the number even if I did.

I paused, scanning every face, when I felt a warm presence behind me.

"Looking for me?" His deep voice caused my eyes to close automatically in delight.

I spun around smiling. "Yes," I breathed.

His blue eyes smiled back, flickering down to the necklace, his heart still sitting at the base of my throat. He blinked, and I saw the sadness I felt mirrored in his eyes, but only for a moment. As if he'd made the same resolution as me, he quickly pushed sadness away. We still had twenty-four hours together.

"Come this way," he said, taking my bag. "I've got us a few chairs near an umbrella."

I followed him past rows of loungers occupied by humans of all shapes and colors smiling, drinking, laughing, or relaxing. It was clearly the end of the week, and while for most, that was cause for celebration, for us, it was a sadness that kept trying to sneak in.

"Wine spritzers," he said, leading me around the lounger.

I laughed. "Why?"

"They're surprisingly refreshing in this heat." He stretched out on a chair, lifting a silicone wine glass and tapping mine. I watched him toss back the sparkling beverage and sipped mine. I didn't want to be fuzzy. I wanted to remember everything.

He rolled to his side, watching as I slid the cover-up down my shoulders. I almost felt shy as his lips curled up slowly in approval. "Red," he murmured.

"It's funny," I said, fumbling with my towel. "I've never paid much attention to the colors I wore. Until now."

His nose curled slightly with his smile, and I couldn't help it. I leaned forward and kissed him. No one here cared. No one here knew either of us. The only two people who did were miles away exploring rock formations (or each other) in Sedona, and all my problems were even further away. I had no reason to hesitate in showing my affections. We could be as free as Elaine and Patrick.

Pausing before I straightened up again, I slid my fingers into the side of his thick, wavy hair.

"I love this," I whispered.

He caught my waist, pulling me to sitting on the side of his chair then he sat up as well, swinging his legs around and pulling me close to his body.

"You can't do things like that," he said, planting his lips against my shoulder. I shivered as he made his way up my neck, behind my ear. "I thought about you all night. I almost knocked on your door."

My pulse beat fire under my skin, and everywhere his lips touched seemed to ignite. The slickness between my thighs had me wanting to lead him into one of the cabanas, where I could slip off my bottoms and straddle his lap. We could easily come together and no one would ever know.

"You could've," I breathed, my eyes closing. "Elaine never came back."

"Patrick's a lucky bastard," he said. But I paused. My expression caused him to laugh. "I only mean he has no reason to hesitate."

"And you do?"

That stopped his progress. He looked into my eyes for a moment, not speaking. Then he said softly. "Everything you've done tells me I do."

I bit my lip looking down. He was right. I'd been secretive and distant, putting up boundaries around questions we couldn't ask, paths we couldn't follow. Even if he didn't know why, he knew I was hiding something, and it was something big enough that no amount of fantastic sex could break down the wall.

"We only have one more day," I said. "Can we stay off that path just a few more hours?"

He nodded. "Of course."

I kissed his lips once more, then I stood and spread out my towel on the second lounger in the sun. Lying back with my aviators on, I took a deep breath. I lifted the glass and took a drink, cooling the fire he'd lit under my skin.

The sun was hot, but it felt good to me. The constant breeze kept it from being unbearable.

"I'm getting in for a bit," he said, and I watched him walk to the pool, his perfect physique turning many heads.

How had I managed to capture his affection? How long could I hold onto it outside this secret oasis in the desert? My situation wasn't forever. Would it be possible to find him once my problems were resolved? Was it realistic to think he might still be available? Waiting for me? Asking him to do so would mean having to explain why, and considering his line of work, that would open a whole kettle of complicated fish.

My eyes squeezed shut, and I lay my head back. I could only conquer one problem at a time. Getting back, I would put my plans in motion, then once everything was complete, perhaps I could pay a visit to the Alexander offices in Princeton. It was a short drive, and if he was as well-known as Elaine said, he should be easy to find.

I took another long sip, finishing my glass, and when I looked up, Derek was headed back in my direction. He was dripping from the pool again and looking so sexy. Without his sunglasses, I could see his eyes travel from my toes, up my calves to my thighs, to my breasts where they lingered before meeting my eyes. The dark blue hadn't faded, and the closer he got, the more I wanted to satisfy his hunger. He sat on his lounger facing me.

"I thought that would cool me," he said.

"Did it?" I asked, studying his expression.

"No." His eyes traveled down my body again.

"What can we do about that?"

At that opening, his eyes snapped back to mine. "My room's the closest."

Without another word, I sat up and slid my cover-up back over my shoulders. His brow relaxed, and he grabbed his shirt off the top of the chair. I picked up my bag and followed him past the rows of sunbathers, admiring the movement of his firm butt as he walked. Every step flexed a different muscle, and I grew tense with anticipation the closer we got to the elevators.

I hoped we'd have the space to ourselves, but no such luck. An elderly patron boarded the lift with us as we made our way to the second floor. It was probably for the best. We might not have made it to our destination otherwise. Room 213 wasn't too far down the hall. I watched as he slid his door key quickly in and out of the silver box, the tension of waiting those final seconds taunted my desire for him.

The door closed behind us, I dropped my bag, and he turned, lifting me against him and bruising my mouth with kisses. My arms were wrapped tightly around his neck, my mouth open and eager to meet his. Tongues collided, and he walked, carrying me to the king-sized bed filling the room. I felt him drop to his knees and opened my eyes as he slid me back on the amazingly soft white linens.

I helped, easing myself to the center, but he stayed at the side, reaching forward and taking hold of my bikini bottoms. In one quick pull they were off. His smile was hungry, and he caught the backs of my knees, pulling my wet opening to his mouth. My head dropped back, and I moaned deeply as his warm tongue slowly circled the little spot that drove me wild. It was hot and gentle then rough and sucking. My hips followed his movements, and when his beard scuffed my skin, I flinched, thrilled by the added sensation. My muscles were so tight, and the little noises he loved were coming from my throat. In two more little pulls, his mouth covering my clit, I was flying. His fingers slipped inside me, and he groaned.

"You're so wet," he said, kissing the inside of my thigh.

"I want you so bad," I moaned. "Please... Don't make me beg."

He stood up fast, slipping down his shorts, and for the first time I saw his enormous cock before it entered me fully erect.

"Oh, god," I hissed, reaching out to wrap my fingers around him. "You're huge."

His lids drooped as my hand slid down his considerable length and then back up it. I couldn't resist. I put the tip into my mouth and sucked. I couldn't take him all in, he was far too big, but I ran my tongue around him, teasing his ridges, enjoying his sharp intake of breath followed by his low moans. I pulled his tip in and out, sucking and taunting him with my tongue, pulsing my hand up and down his shaft. His hips rocked slightly as he made a low groan, gently touching my cheek. After only a few moments, he caught my hair and held my face back.

"I need to be inside you now." One glance at the large muscle I'd been playing with told me why. A tiny white drop escaped his slit, and I shivered knowing what that meant.

Quickly unfastening my bikini top, I moved back just as he joined me, pulling me down and filling me with his size.

"Ooh," I moaned as once again my body was stretched in the most delicious way possible. My orgasm that had only cooled slightly as I played with him came raging back with every thrust.

He groaned and rolled me on top of him, clutching my buttocks hard and lifting me, gripping me up and plunging me back down. I gasped, reaching forward, placing my palms flat against the headboard, rocking my clit against his shaft. The friction had me blazing and tight. His groans were animal and wild.

In my position, leaning forward, my breasts teased in his face, and his tiny sucks and bites registered directly between my legs. I shook with pleasure. That intense orgasm was on the brink of bursting through me. Two more impossibly deep thrusts and shudders exploded down my limbs.

"Derek…" I moaned, and he groaned low in response, still pushing into me. I gasped, my core muscles spasming around his enormous cock again and again, my fingers digging into the headboard as the orgasm radiated through my lower body.

He rocked his hips two more times, going deep into me and groaning loudly in release. Then I collapsed in his huge, strong arms, completely spent. He wrapped them around me, holding me tight against him as we rolled to the side. Our hearts pounded, our breath came so fast. My eyes were closed, and I felt his soft lips kissing my brows, my lids, moving to my nose, down to just gently touching my lips. I blinked slowly, and he smiled.

"You come in the most spectacular way for me," he said.

My first instinct was to be self-conscious, but he kissed me again.

"I've never made love like this," I said softly. "I've never felt it so intensely."

He kissed me lightly again. "It's amazing. You're amazing."

I was wrapped in the circle of his arms, feeling as safe as if I were in a cocoon. "I could say the same to you."

"I only do what you let me. If you weren't into it, none of this would happen."

I thought about that a moment. What was it about him that conjured this wild, sexual side of me I'd never known existed? The side that would follow a stranger to a dark, secluded patio for insane, animal fucking. Or into a family bathroom. That had me screaming in his bed? Was it just chemistry? Was it his confidence? Was it the way he was so sure of what I wanted and so ready to give it to me? I didn't have the answers. I only knew I'd lose something truly major when we said goodbye.

"I guess that's true," I finally said. "But you know exactly how to lead me there. And you're not just willing, you're eager to take me."

"Why the hell wouldn't I be?"

My brow lined, and this time when our eyes met, our expressions were serious, as if we both knew what was on the line tomorrow. I sighed, lowering my cheek to his chest, tracing my finger through the light sprinkling of hair there.

He continued lightly kissing my forehead, my cheek, and I drifted to sleep wishing that I never had to leave this wonderful spot.

CHAPTER 9 – THE END OF THE WEEK

I stayed in Derek's room all night, and we made love several more times, passionately, gently, each time savoring our final moments together, until at last we *had* to sleep. When I opened my eyes to the sunlight bursting over the low hills, my heart broke. It was here. The end of the week.

Derek was still asleep behind me, his strong arms wrapped tightly around my waist as if he could protect me from what was waiting for my return if I let him. I knew he would, and I was certain he'd do a damn good job. But if that had been what I'd wanted, I'd have gone to the police a long time ago.

No, what I was dealing with I wanted to handle myself, and only involve the very few who absolutely had to know. I took a deep breath, thinking of the packing I hadn't done. Of the plane I had to catch in a few hours.

I stretched, placing my hands on his forearms and gently moving them apart. He released me, rolling onto his back, and I sat up, glancing over my shoulder to see him blinking at the ceiling. Then he turned to look at me. A sad smile in his eyes.

"Every morning this week I woke up wishing you were in my bed," he said, sliding my long dark curls off my back. He sat up and kissed the top of my shoulder, then my smiling lips. His hand slid to my waist then up, cupping my breast. Tingles rose along my legs at his touch, but I was out of time.

"I have to get back to my room," I sighed. "I haven't even begun to pack."

He kissed the top of my shoulder again, wrapping his arms around my waist. "I wish there was something I could do. Start the week over somehow."

I slid forward and picked up my bathing suit, wishing I'd packed at least a dress or something to wear for the walk back to the spa side.

"I keep thinking of all the missed opportunities," I smiled, sliding my cover up over my shoulders and leaning forward to kiss him. "Who needs food? Sleep? Manicures? I should've been with you."

He laughed and tried to hold onto me, but I stepped back. "And now I have to go." But as I said the words, the pain twisted in my chest.

His brow creased, and he stood, stepping into his discarded swim trunks. "Let me walk you back."

"We'll look ridiculous in swimsuits so early in the morning," I tried to laugh. To think of anything to ease the intense misery growing inside me. But it didn't work.

"I couldn't care less." He slipped the tee back over his head and took my hand, picking up my bag.

We caught the elevator down and then walked out into the still-cool morning. Neither of us spoke, but our hands were clasped tightly like two teenagers at the end of a summer romance. Once we reached the entrance to the spa hotel, he stopped and faced me.

"Last name?" he asked, but I shook my head no. I didn't want him investigating me. I didn't want him knowing. He exhaled. "I've been thinking. Maryland's not so far."

"I'll be going back to Wilmington soon," I said quietly.

He nodded, and something flickered in his eyes, thoughtful if still sad. "That's good. I hope you'll be happier there."

A line creased my brow. "What do you mean?"

"That first night I saw you in the bar," he paused, as if searching for the right words. "You were so sad."

I relaxed. "If I'm happy now, I have you to thank."

He reached forward and slid a curl off my cheek. "Thank you," he murmured.

I remembered his odd gratitude the few first times we'd made love. "Why did you? Thank me, I mean. Those first times."

"I knew you were doing something unusual, something you'd probably never have done." He paused a moment, choosing his words. "I kept holding my breath, waiting for you to push me away or make me stop, and when you didn't..."

"Thank you," I whispered.

He smiled. "You're amazing. And you let me have you."

He had no idea how much I'd let him have. For a moment we were quiet. I hated this goodbye so much. Suddenly, he reached forward and caught both my hands. He took a deep breath and looked straight into my eyes as if he'd just made a decision.

"I never expected things to go this way. To get so involved so fast." He paused, glancing briefly at our clasped hands. I started to speak, but he continued. "And then I said a week, as if I could just do this one-week thing…"

My stomach was so tight, but I only blinked, waiting to hear him out.

"We both have lives back home," he continued, "and maybe you can't share your life with me now. But I'd take your call anytime." He was holding my hands so securely. "I hope this goodbye isn't—"

"Forever," I said softly with him. His childhood game drifted through my memory.

My eyes were warm, and he stepped forward, releasing my hands and cupping my cheeks as he kissed me gently, then deeply. *When we see each other again, I thought, this is what we'll do.* I placed my hands over his, opening my mouth to him for the last time, fighting tears with everything I had. I didn't want his last memory to be of me crying.

When he stepped back, he touched the heart at my throat. "I meant what I wrote."

I lifted it in my fingers. "I'll take good care of it."

* * *

The plane ride back to Maryland was miserable. Elaine and I were both quiet, thoughtful, and I could tell her parting with Patrick had been emotional, too. But in contrast, they'd exchanged contact information and a promise to keep in touch. I couldn't do that.

In Atlanta, we parted ways, her headed east and me north. We hugged each other, and it was comforting to know we were close enough to be in this silent place of misery together and not have to question it, pick it apart, or even discuss it.

"So our next trip," she said, her voice quiet. "I'll start planning it the minute I get unpacked."

I nodded, my smile tight. Tears were close in my eyes, but my friend didn't seem to notice. I could tell she had her own tears to manage.

"Have a great start of the school year," I said, squeezing her hands, not wanting to let her go.

She hugged me close. "I'll be so glad when you're finally home."

"Me, too," I breathed. "It shouldn't be long now. I'll keep you posted."

With that we went our separate ways—at least temporarily.

The entire trip to Baltimore, I couldn't rest. I couldn't read. I only stared out the little window thinking of Derek and missing him so much. I was alone, headed back to my unfinished business, and Sloan had been calling the entire time. He was certain to be furious, and when he was furious...

I inhaled deeply as the announcer began telling us about the descent into the metropolitan airport. I collected my purse, which held the heart necklace in my wallet. I hadn't worn it because I'd have to explain, but I was keeping it safe and secure, hoping against hope that I'd be able to find him again. And that when I did, it might actually work as well in real life as it had in our little one-week summer oasis.

* * *

Sloan's car was waiting for me when I emerged from baggage claim. I wouldn't have even seen it if Hal, his Asian driver, hadn't called out to me.

"Mr. Reynolds said you'll be needing a ride home," he said with a smile, taking my suitcase.

"H-he did?" Instantly my stomach clenched. If Sloan knew when I was arriving and which airline, he must've found out where I went. I wondered just how much he knew. Derek and I'd thrown discretion to the wind our last day at the pool, and my insides tensed at the thought of what Sloan might do if he found out I'd taken a lover.

"Yes, Mrs. Reynolds," Hal was still smiling. "He said you wouldn't be expecting me."

I exhaled deeply and felt my shoulders drop. I was back. "Thank you, Hal. And I'm not going by 'Mrs. Reynolds' anymore. I've told you that."

"Yes, ma'am," he said, but I could tell he was only humoring me. No telling what Sloan had told his staff about me. Probably that I had mental problems. Or at the very least, that the whole thing was my fault.

I took one last look over my shoulder, back at the concourse, and then blinked away the mist in my eyes as I turned and followed the black-uniformed employee to my husband's limo waiting to take me "home."

CHAPTER 10 – CUT THE TIES

No one greeted me when Hal dropped me at the front door. If I'd expected Sloan to be waiting with a snarl, I'd forgotten his style. He preferred to play it cool, aloof, much too busy for the childish behavior of his trophy wife. Then he'd strike for revenge once I'd forgotten I'd even done anything.

I hated him.

I slowly climbed the marble staircase to my room. Yes, we had separate rooms. This enormous house with a conservatory, a ballroom, and two formal dining areas—it was like something out of the fucking *Sound of Music*—had plenty of bedrooms, and my husband and I had only shared one for about two months when we moved here a year ago.

He'd complained it was too hot. He didn't have enough room. He suggested we get a California king-sized bed, but it was too late. The damage had been done, and I just wanted my own space. He snored anyway.

Today my luggage would be delivered to my private suite on the east wing of the mansion. The staff would wait for me to unload it and sort my clothes between the dirty and clean. Laundry was sent to an outside service then returned pressed and folded. The housekeeper, Mrs. Widlow met me at the top of the stairs. Her sleek grey hair hung in a straight bob that never moved, and as always, she wore a pantsuit and matching scarf. Today the suit was puce, the scarf lavender.

"Did you have a nice trip, Mrs. Reynolds?" she said.

"It was very relaxing," I answered. "And I've asked not to be called by that name any more."

"Of course, ma'am," she said.

Just like Hal.

They were Sloan's staff, and like the rest, she didn't give a shit what I said. Whatever Mr. Reynolds told them was law.

I continued making my way to my suite. The first time Sloan brought me here five years ago, when I was only twenty-six, everything about his huge mansion knocked my small-town socks off, from the grounds to the stables to the garage filled with all sorts of antique cars. Of course, at that time, it was still his father's mansion.

Back then, the only thing more impressive to me than this house was that Sloan Reynolds, Princeton graduate, mogul, inheritor of his father's export business, had taken an interest in me. I still hadn't figured that puzzler out.

I was simply an ambitious marketing major based on the Carolina coast but participating in workshops at big-wig universities hoping to make bank by snagging some major clients. I was freelance, but in this digital age, I had dreams of managing the world from my hammock on the beach.

My future husband had been on campus that day delivering a check or having his butt kissed by some needy department chair. He'd spotted me making my pitch and invited me to lunch. He was older, but at the time, he was still sexy to me. He was experienced and worldly — rich, smooth, and in control. He took me to the best restaurants, ordered the best wines. The rest was history.

Five years as Mrs. Sloan Reynolds had left me *very* cynical. About everything.

The first months of our marriage were good — he was kind to me, and we enjoyed being together. Then slowly his interest faded. He seemed to enjoy my company less and less, and he started taking more and longer trips back to Baltimore.

When we relocated, his traveling increased. He said he had to take over his father's schedule, meeting with investors and potential customers in far-off locations. I was never invited to join him, and I later found out why.

He'd asked me to put my marketing career on hold and take his mother's place on her many local charity boards, auxiliaries, and civic associations. Of course, I agreed — anything to help with the transition. His father's death changed everything.

So my marketing business dwindled, and I made few client contacts in the city. Instead, I did what the wives of the super-wealthy did. I attended meetings, had teas, cut ribbons. The only problem was, I didn't want to give up my career. I didn't want to be a lady who lunched. I didn't even know how to play tennis.

I confess — I blamed myself a little for our marriage's "failure to thrive," as the counseling booklets called it. Sloan had swept me off my feet, and he had style. And drivers. And cache into all the best places. But apart from that, we had little in common. I told myself it didn't matter. We would grow into those things.

The opposite happened.

And as if to hasten the decline, our sex life never got off the ground. When we did have intercourse, he at least seemed satisfied. He gasped and groaned and got off, and I sort of followed along. But his hands never drifted below my waist, he didn't like blow jobs, didn't give me head. We would have one disappointing moment, and then months would go by before we'd try again.

Eventually, I quit trying.

I was depressed as hell when I found the receipt in his pants pocket. He'd spent two thousand dollars on a Jessica Black. It only took a few Google searches for me to discover Ms. Black was a high-end call-girl.

He told me it meant nothing. He was having a crisis. He needed to "feel" something again. And after all, she was just a "faceless whore." None of that mattered. I just wanted to be done with it. I wanted to go back to Wilmington and resume my career in marketing. I wanted to restart my freelance business, forget the whole marriage charade, and get back to what made me happy.

Six months had passed, and we'd tried counseling, therapy. I'd even talked to my mom, although I knew her advice before she offered it: All marriages hit rough patches, give it time. It had all been well and good until the night he decided he was tired of waiting for me to "get over it." Until the night he changed everything.

After that I never wanted to see him again. I filed for divorce two weeks ago—the week before Elaine had taken me to Scottsdale for our spa retreat. I hadn't had a chance to tell anyone but her before we left. I hadn't even had a chance to plan my exit strategy.

As it was, I still had to collect enough money for a deposit on my own place. I still had to decide how I would live—that is, unless I decided to come clean and move in with my mother until I got on my feet again. I wanted to save that option as the very last resort. I still had a few small marketing jobs in the works, and once those clients paid, I'd pack up and leave Baltimore.

Those were the details I was working out when I left for Scottsdale and met Derek.

Derek opened my eyes. He turned my body inside out, and then he set everything on fire. But at the same time, nothing had changed. Derek might've shown me I wasn't to blame, that I could fall in love, that my life could get better. But before any of it could be realized, I had to finish here. I had to get back on my own two feet.

I was still unpacking my suitcase and pondering closure when my soon-to-be ex-husband found me. As I expected, he was not in an understanding mood.

He was ready to get to the bottom of my unannounced trip.

CHAPTER 11 – PORTFOLIO DIVERSITY

Sloan breezed into the room as if finding me here was the last thing he'd expected to happen—as if he hadn't sent his driver to pick me up at the airport. My pulse sped up. My back was to him, and without turning, I cautiously lifted my hand to one of the small top drawers of my dresser. Sliding it open, I casually felt beneath my lingerie, locating the canister of pepper spray now hidden there.

"Well, look what the cat dragged in," he said, dropping lightly onto my bed. He was long and lean, dressed in expensive tan slacks and a pale blue button-down shirt. His light-brown hair was losing its battle against the grey, and I remembered a time when his age had made him seem distinguished to me. "I do love your flair for the dramatic, my dear. Have me served then disappear for a week. *Brava!*"

His words also reminded me of a time when I'd debated whether my husband might be gay. The prospect had softened me toward him. I'd wanted to help him come out, let him know it was okay. He'd grown up in a time and in a world not so understanding of alternate lifestyles. Then I discovered his penchant for prostitutes. Jessica Black had only been the first of many contact slips I'd found. No, it seemed his only problem was having sex with his wife.

"Elaine called and invited me on a spa retreat," I said, keeping my voice calm. I continued unpacking, silently waiting for him to make his next move. "But you already know that, don't you?"

"Spa retreat? Why didn't you tell me," he had the nerve to act hurt. "You know I enjoy a good massage as much as the next guy."

He enjoyed a happy ending. He probably had masseuses all over town ready to jerk him off for a modest fee. The thought made me sick.

"It was more of a friend getaway." The tension was making my shoulders ache. I wanted him to say whatever he'd come to say or do and leave. "You would've been bored."

"No doubt of that." Then as if he'd somehow lost interest, he sat up and went to the door. "As I said, some third-rate lawyer sent your papers. A James Pettigrew or something?"

"James Perry." He knew damn well my lawyer's name.

"Perry, right." He paused in the doorway. "I sent them on to Thomas for a good once-over. Can't have my lady screwing me now, can I."

It would be the first time in a long time, I thought bitterly, but I wouldn't take his bait.

Thomas was Sloan's self-serving lawyer, and if there was anything wrong with the divorce papers, he'd find it. The shocker for both of them would come when they discovered I just wanted out. No alimony, no settlement, just freedom.

"Look them over as much as you need," I said with a smile. "I'm sure you'll find they're completely to your benefit."

He nodded. "Then, welcome home Melissa."

I didn't reply. This was not my home.

* * *

Once I had finished unpacking, I walked down the hall to my study. The office was also a library, and when I'd first visited this wing last year, I'd been thrilled with all the books I could read. Little did I know, reading was all I'd end up doing. A desk was placed in one corner, and I saw my small, silver Macbook lying there. I'd left it behind on my trip, not wanting anything that reminded me of Baltimore. As if I could escape that easily.

Tonight, I went to it, lifted the cover and opened the browser. It had only been a day, and already the pain gripped my chest so hard, it hurt to breathe. Quickly I typed in "Derek Alexander" and "private investigator."

Moments later a page of links popped up with the one I sought right at the top. Alexander & Knight, LLC. I glanced quickly at the door then leaned forward, looking as far down the hallway as I could see. No one was coming.

Holding my breath, I clicked on the link. Instantly, I was taken to a plain but professional-looking business site with an A&K logo over an exterior shot of what must be their offices in Princeton. One of the small links across the top said "About Us," and again, my heart clenched as I clicked on it.

The screen changed and there he was. A tiny gasp escaped my lips when I saw his face. It was a professionally posed shot—him in a suit, all-business, just the smallest hint of a smile. His blue eyes seemed to glow, and a knot tightened at the base of my throat. He was gorgeous. I reached out to touch the screen lightly with trembling fingers when I realized I wasn't alone. Quickly I closed the notebook and looked up to see Mrs. Widlow standing in the doorway.

"Mr. Reynolds said he'd be having his supper out," she said, not seeming to notice my suspicious behavior. "When would you like yours?"

I cleared my throat. "If it's not too much trouble, I'd be happy with just a sandwich in my bedroom."

"No trouble at all," the housekeeper said, nodding before she turned to leave.

Once she was definitely away, I slowly opened the computer again. The screen blinked on, and he was still there. I leaned my face on my hand and studied his image a few moments. He was just as sexy in a suit and tie as he'd been in casual attire—maybe more. A hot tear slid down my nose as his last words flooded my memory. He'd take my call anytime.

I wanted to call him right now. Just to hear his voice again. I took a deep breath and navigated his website. I was impressed by how many services they offered. The financial institution security package was listed most prominently, but they also had plans for identity theft and general investigative work.

Patrick's page listed services including missing persons and domestic issues. I wondered how many of those cases they even took. Neither of them mentioned that line of work, and it seemed the online banking and finance was their primary focus.

I shook my head. As a small business owner, I was all too familiar with diversifying one's portfolio just in case, for backup. I clicked back over to Derek's page, and the image of his face again shot pain straight to my chest. I pressed my lips together, swallowing the lump in my throat. Once more I ran the back of my finger down the screen, remembering his kisses, his strong arms holding me. I felt so safe sleeping in them. Tears were multiplying, but I blinked them away. And with a sigh, I slid the mouse forward and clicked on the little red X.

* * *

My mother's voice held its usual note of concern. Ever since I'd first told her Sloan and I were having serious problems, she'd urged me wait. And every time she did, I almost told her why that was no longer an option.

But I couldn't.

I couldn't bear saying what had happened out loud. Especially not to her. The very thought of telling her everything made my stomach roil. If my father were still alive, it would've been even worse.

"So you're moving home," she said. "I guess you have to do what you think is best."

"I've spent as much time as I can trying to make it work, Mom," I said quietly, keeping my voice calm. "Nothing's changing. Things are actually getting worse as time passes."

"Disappearing for a week without a word certainly can't be helping with the reconciliation effort."

My jaw clenched. "I didn't disappear without a word, I just didn't tell him where I was going."

"The results are the same," she exhaled lightly. "So when do you expect to be here?"

"I'm not sure," I said, toying with the sandwich on my supper tray. I wasn't very hungry. "My goal is to find a place and not have to bother you, but it just depends—"

"You're not bothering me, honey. I just want you to be sure you're not doing something you'll regret."

"I'm not," I said, pressing my lips together.

My work with Sloan's family had kept me so busy the first half of the year, I hadn't been able to visit home. Then after the incident, I hadn't wanted to visit. I didn't feel strong enough to see anyone, much less my super-perceptive mother. She would've demanded I do what I didn't really want to.

As it was, I had to be patient with her ignorance. "Just give me one more week," I said. "I'll know something definite then."

"The door's open if you need it."

"Thanks so much, Mom."

We hung up the phone, and I stretched back on my bed. Moving in with Mom was my absolute last resort, but I figured spreading a safety net couldn't hurt. Sloan had become so unpredictable, and now that he had the divorce papers, I wasn't sure what he'd do.

Two months ago, fueled by my determination to get out, I'd drummed up business with two local clients—a suburban strip mall needing a back to school campaign, and a downtown bakery wanting to test the cupcake waters. Neither of them were particularly wealthy clients, but they weren't poor either. I'd sent invoices to them the week before Elaine and I had left for Scottsdale.

My hope was they'd come through and I could go straight to my own place in Wilmington.

Either way, I had to start looking for somewhere to live and transitioning my contact information. The only thing holding me back now were the details. Details I'd see about first thing tomorrow.

CHAPTER 12 – A LIST OF NAMES

Bea's Fancy Cakes was located in an older part of downtown that was now a few blocks off the major pedestrian thoroughfares. The owner, affectionately known as "Aunt Bea," had provided cakes to downtown businesses and residents for almost thirty years, but her sales had dropped as traffic patterns had rotated away from her address.

When she contacted me about helping her market a new line of cupcakes, my enthusiasm lifted her spirits so much, we'd become friends as well as partners. It also earned me a free sample every visit. Today, I hoped it would land an early payment on my invoice, but I knew I had to approach the topic gingerly. She was old-fashioned, and I hoped not overextended.

"That one's a new recipe," she said, sliding over my cupcake *du jour* as she assisted a customer.

"Candy corn. I'm testing it for the Halloween market."

Aunt Bea was a fabulous baker, and adding a trendy cupcake line had been a stroke of brilliance to solve her location woes. We simply had to remind the public she was here and convince the downtown foot-traffic to take a slight detour on their way back to the office after lunch. Extending her business hours also picked up after-work employees who'd forgotten a birthday, or Valentine's Day, or their anniversary. We'd watched with glee as the clientele had grown from one or two customers a day to tens and twenties. I smiled, satisfied as I lifted the little orange, yellow, and white candy off the top of my confection. I'd helped somebody during my time here in a meaningful way.

"It smells exactly right," I said, inspecting the golden-yellow ombre frosting before taking a bite. "Mmm..." I couldn't stop a groan of delight as the lightly sweet, toasted-butter flavor filled my mouth. "It's perfect!"

Bea grinned and pulled out a pink and white polka-dot box for the waiting male customer. "Saw the recipe in one of those parent magazines and just tweaked it a bit," she said. "I might make an entire cake from it."

"This will fly off the shelves."

My trip to the desert had coincided with Labor Day, which meant Halloween season had begun. Black and orange ornamentation, cats, and pumpkins were popping up everywhere. It was my favorite time of year with the air growing cooler and the leaves changing colors.

Elaine's return home had put her in full back-to-school mode, and I hadn't talked to her since we'd parted at the airport. I wondered how things were going with her and Patrick, and immediately, I considered sending her a box of this heaven.

"Three red wine velvet, and three tiramisu," Bea repeated, making a note of the waiting customer's order before filling the box. "So what brings you downtown?"

Chewing my lip, I waited as she rang up the fellow, who took the box and hastened to the door. Aunt Bea was short and round, and with her little bun, she actually did resemble the television icon she was nicknamed for.

We were alone at last, and I had to act quickly before another customer entered the bakery. But I didn't want to rush her into a no. "Well," I started, swallowing my heart down. "I'm moving back to Wilmington."

"What!" Her thin eyebrows pulled together quickly as they rose. "I don't understand. What about…?"

"It's sort of a complicated situation. You see, Sloan and I are getting a divorce." I played with the wax paper lying flat at the base of my half-eaten cupcake.

"Oh, honey," Bea walked around the glass case and pulled me into a hug. "Is there anything I can do?"

"Actually," I inhaled her sugary scent and just said it. "Well, I hoped you might be in a position to pay the invoice I sent over a little early."

For a moment, we were both quiet. Her lips pressed together, and I felt a bead of sweat trickle down my back.

"I'm so sorry to ask you," I continued. "It's just that I'm not sure of my new address, and it would make wrapping up my business here… easier."

She shook her head. "I hate to see you go. Mr. Reynolds was such a good man, and you seemed like a perfect addition to that family."

A lump rose in my throat. Sloan's elderly father had been revered as something like a saint by all the downtown residents. He'd held local business in the area through economic ups and downs, and he was a kind man. Despite his son.

But more than that—her words brought me healing. For so long, I'd blamed myself for being a fool, for not seeing the real Sloan before I'd married him. After the incident, I'd assumed I'd been blinded by his family name and the luxury of the life he'd offered. But Bea's words confirmed what I'd believed six years ago, in the beginning. Sloan's father *had* been kind. I *had* seemed to belong. At first.

I'd never dreamed such a dark underbelly could be lurking on that idyllic family life. In that moment, I got a bit of my self-esteem back.

"And I know you would be a great partner in downtown development," she continued. Her voice was tentative. I knew she was trying not to offend me. "I hate to lose my best publicity girl."

My heart filled despite its inner turmoil. Her words were so kind, and I was sure if my situation weren't so bleak, she'd be right. My life might be so different here. But it wasn't, and I was ready to leave this place.

Her words also reminded me why Sloan went on the attack when I'd said I wanted a divorce. Why he was so worried about what public accusations I might make, and why he was so ready to shift the blame for all of it to me.

He had the most to lose in this town, and he knew better than to shit where he ate. If my story became The Story, it would ruin him. He was on the defense, and it was a scary place to have him. He was wicked when cornered.

"I know," I said quietly, adopting my usual line.

"But it's just not working out, and we've decided it was a mistake. We'll be happier apart."

She pressed her lips into a smile as she squeezed my upper arm. "Well, that's too bad." I watched her walk back to the register, quietly holding my breath, hoping she'd help me. "Would you be able to give me a week? Is that a problem?"

I quietly exhaled, small tears touching my eyes. "No problem at all!" I did my best not to dance around her bakery—she wouldn't understand. "And thank you so much. I hope we can continue working together."

"How could we do that?" Her face lined.

"It's the digital age! You'd be amazed what all I can do from the comfort of my laptop."

She shook her head, but immediately smiled at the female customer walking through the door. "These computers. They've changed everything."

"Thanks so much, Aunt Bea." I gathered the rest of my cupcake as I headed for the door.

One week. One more week, and I'd be gone. I could feel my lungs straining in anticipation. Soon I'd be able to breathe freely again.

* * *

After that, I was in full apartment-hunting mode. I focused my search on small condos near the beach. The chances were great I wouldn't find anything I could afford, but I was optimistic. I even started collecting moving supplies.

I'd only seen Sloan once, naturally when I was about to carry two broken-down boxes up the large staircase to my room. I tensed, waiting for how he would respond. The muscle in his jaw tightened, but he didn't say a word. He simply continued to his study and closed the door. I quietly jogged up the steps and then hurried to my solitary quarters in the east wing.

We hadn't dined together, we hadn't had a single conversation since the one in my bedroom the night I'd returned home. I was not complaining. If I never spoke to him again, it would be too soon. But I was nervous. He hadn't agreed to let me go, and he didn't like being crossed.

My nerves were tied up and confused between my growing anticipation of freedom combined with the tension of watching for anything from Sloan. Before Scottsdale, I'd been used to the nonstop pressure, the invisible weights pushing down on my shoulders all the time. But that week-long reprieve had shown me how toxic Baltimore was, and it was all I could do to stay here and wrap up my business.

* * *

Alone in my room, I opened a spreadsheet to compile a list of names. I'd started this once before, back when I was first launching my freelance business. My potential client list. A few of the entries from those days might still be interested in working with me, but the chances were better after all this time they'd established relationships with other providers. Still, I'd send them all my contact information once I'd set up my new identity in Wilmington.

Thinking of possibilities, my eyes drifted to the Internet browser window. It had become a guilty habit of mine, a nighttime indulgence. My eyes flickered to my door—no one was coming in here tonight—I clicked on the icon and hastily typed in the now-memorized address. Two clicks, and Derek's face appeared on the screen, jolting my heart with a dose of happiness.

I was like a teenage girl gazing at pictures of my favorite boy band. My cheek rested on my hand, and I reached forward to trace the line of his face with my finger as joy pulsed through me with each heartbeat. I still remembered his scent. Closing my eyes, I could still feel the touch of his lips against mine. Only a little time had passed since he'd nuzzled his face into my shoulder, kissed my neck, lifted me against his firm torso. His kiss was my moment, the thing I held onto that helped me know this pain wasn't forever. My lips warmed with longing for the day when I saw him again, when he'd cover my mouth with his and take me.

Rolling onto my back, eyes still closed, I allowed my memory to conjure the sensation of his mouth searching every part of my body. Instantly, I grew wet. My hand slid between my legs as my core filled with heat remembering his mouth being where my hand was now, tasting, exploring, pulling my smaller lips with his. My upper arms pressed my breasts together, and I took us back to our little box. The night he'd held me on his lap, entering me from behind, huge and full. His enormous cock pressed inside, thrusting deeply, rubbing every sensitive place between my legs so well. Driving me crazy.

His hand gripped my stomach, holding me firmly against his chest, easily lifting me up and down. Oh, god, he'd felt so good. A shiver moved through me as my fingers followed the path his larger ones had taken. His phantom whiskers tickled my back, warm lips moving from my neck to my shoulders. He pushed faster, harder, filling me completely, thrusting deeper... a little moan slipped from my lips and my thighs shook with the orgasm his memory provoked. Rolling onto my stomach, I moaned again into the pillow, but a hollow ache reminded me how much I missed the real thing. Memories were nice, but nothing matched his body against mine, his lips on my skin, his cock buried deep inside me.

Several moments passed as I waited, eyes closed, breathing deeply. Calm gradually returned, and with it came that flicker of hope I held so dearly. The hope I'd held when we said goodbye outside the resort.

Mist was in my eyes and my stomach tightened at the memory of his words. He'd take my call anytime. Did he think of me this way? Was he waiting for my call, dreaming of our reunion the way I was?

Moving back to my still-open spreadsheet, I quickly typed fourteen letters and ten digits. At the top of my list of names was his.

CHAPTER 13 – NEVER AGAIN

The week was almost up, and I could barely breathe waiting for the day to arrive. I was like a convict waiting for my pardon. Every day, I snatched the mail the instant it was delivered, rapidly flipping through the envelopes, straining for my name.

The strip mall had paid their bill, which allowed me to put a large down-payment on a one-bedroom condo near the coast that would be my home. I'd lucked into an amazing deal and jumped on it. I was almost giddy with anticipation. I couldn't wait to be there, but the remainder of my money was eaten up in deposits for turning on services and in rent for a mini storage facility for my things. I needed Aunt Bea's outstanding check to carry me through the transition.

Every day I waited, hoping for that envelope bearing my name, but every day I was disappointed. It never appeared. It was too late to go back and set up direct deposit for her payment—not that my elderly client would've even understood the concept. But I'd learned my lesson going forward. All future accounts would have a direct pay mandate.

The added tension of waiting for Sloan's backlash only increased my anxiety. At least no one back home knew about my pending return. I wasn't sure I could handle nonstop questions of when I'd be in town. My former landlord knew I was returning, as he'd helped me compile the information needed to purchase my new condo. Elaine would've been tripping over herself to help, of course, but for most people, returning after a divorce wasn't cause for celebration. I was happy to be free, but despite it all, I wanted to leave my past in the past. I would tell my friends as little as I could to satisfy their concerned curiosity.

Another day of waiting was another day of taking boxes to the delivery service. I had all my things sent to a mini storage facility in Wilmington that agreed to hold them until I arrived. I did it partly to keep Sloan from knowing my business—if he were investigating—and partly because it was easier than trying to hire a truck. I'd handle an in-town move once I was back home, but I was doing my best to keep all my plans under wraps.

So my delay had an unanticipated upside. My existence here was almost completely packed and moved. It was amazing how little a human being actually needed when possessions were stripped down to the essentials.

* * *

Stepping into the library that evening, I replaced the hardback I'd never read. I turned slowly, inhaling the scent of books and studying the shelves. My dreams of living in this place had been so different from my reality.

Shaking my head, I left the room. No sense going back down that path. I was moving forward now. And I was ready to curl into bed for my nighttime ritual.

I did not expect to see Sloan standing in my doorway. "I see you're determined to go through with this," he said, a stern line piercing the skin between his brows.

He wore grey slacks, and his top button was open. His hair was disheveled, and I saw his chest rise and fall. His agitated expression was too familiar, and quickly my mind counted the days. How long had it been since he'd traveled? Why was he here now? My throat went dry.

"I am," I managed to say.

He stepped forward, and I stepped to the side, anticipating the need to move quickly.

"Why are you doing this, Melissa? What could you possibly want that you don't have here?"

My eyes widened. "Is that a joke?"

"Not at all. You live like a queen."

I shook my head not knowing where to begin answering his question. As if he even deserved an answer. "We really don't know each other at all, do we?"

"Apparently not," he said, entering my room. I followed trying to get around him to my dresser drawer, but he stayed between me and my one small protection.

"If we did," he continued, "you'd know how much I detest divorce."

I flashed at his attempt to take some moral high ground. "I don't believe in husbands raping their wives."

He rolled his eyes, waving a hand. "I didn't rape you."

"You tried," I snapped.

"It was a misunderstanding. And anyway, some women like it rough."

The rage I'd held inside for over three months roared in my chest, choking me with its ferocity. I cleared my throat, shaking my head, trying to stay calm. "Are you saying some women like being beaten?"

He leveled his brown eyes on mine. "You threw the first punch."

Shudders kept moving through my body. We'd never discussed that night since it happened, and my resistance to talking about it had left me unprepared for how it would affect me if I did. I wasn't sure I could do this alone.

"You tried to rape me," I said, my voice small, my throat painfully tight. "I was only defending myself."

"Regardless," he continued, as if enjoying my discomfort. "*You* started it. *I* finished it. And I bet you never hit me again."

I turned to face my open door, ready to run and not caring if I took anything with me. I wanted to leave this place for good. Tonight.

As if reading my mind, Sloan quickly moved from my dresser to catch my upper arm, jerking me against his body. "You're *my* wife," he hissed in my ear. "You belong to *me*. No matter what you think you're going to do, that fact will always remain."

Tears spilled onto my cheeks. I couldn't catch my breath, and a hiccup jerked my shoulders. "Please let me go," I whimpered.

His grip remained tight on my arm. "I'll never let you go. And even when you're gone, I'll know every step you take. You are never out of my reach."

My heart hammered, and I tried to keep my shoulders straight. I refused to cower to him. Still, my body instinctively shrank from his touch. I hadn't wanted to believe he might hurt me again. But now I knew he would.

He loosened his hold and shoved me back before stalking out of my room, slamming the door behind him. I dashed to it, quickly turning the lock, knowing it wouldn't keep him out if he wanted back in.

I ran to my closet and pulled out a suitcase, throwing every outfit I could get my hands on into it as sobs gasped from my throat, fear strangling my voice. The check might be in the mail, but I wasn't waiting anymore.

* * *

I slept with my door locked and the pepper spray clutched in my hand all night. I didn't want to take my car—I didn't want to take anything that might be considered community property. Late in the night, once I'd calmed down, I called Elaine and asked if she could come and get me now. I didn't want to tell her why or scare her, but she knew something was wrong. She said she'd be on the road first thing in the morning. I only had to survive six more hours before we'd be gone. Six hours of acting like nothing was coming. I wasn't sure if I could pull it off.

All night my mind kept running to Derek as I tossed and turned, unable to sleep. One thing Sloan had said troubled me—that even when I was gone he knew every step I took, that I was never out of his reach. When Hal was waiting for me at the airport, I'd mistakenly assumed Sloan had figured out where I went. I thought he'd weaseled the information from my mom or found a stray email on my Macbook. Now I knew the truth. He hadn't figured it out. Clearly, he was having me watched.

The perfect person who could help me with this was Derek. If Sloan had hired a private investigator to track me, Derek would know exactly how to handle the situation. It was possible he might even know the person or be able to find him or her easily. The only problem was I didn't want to involve Derek in my disgusting backstory. With everything in me, I didn't want him to know what Sloan had done. Partly because I was afraid if he knew, he wouldn't want me anymore. He'd think I was too damaged, or maybe he'd believe Sloan. He'd think I started it and what happened was my fault. I shuddered at the thought.

But if Sloan was having me watched, and I tried to see Derek, it would all come out anyway. I cringed at the prospect. My story was so humiliating and awful. I wouldn't blame Derek if he wanted to walk, knowing I had a psycho ex-husband lurking around. The pain of these thoughts kept me troubled all night.

* * *

By morning, I'd formulated a plan. What if there was a way I could find out who was working with Sloan on my own? What if I could talk to the person, reason with him or her, or even pay the person off somehow? Maybe I could solve my problem without Derek ever having to know...

Bolstered by the idea, I crept to my door and unlocked it. It was ten. Elaine would be two hours into her drive if she'd gotten on the road by eight like she'd said she would. It gave me just enough time to try and investigate. I waited, listening. My end of the giant mansion was completely quiet.

I crept down the hallway to the main staircase, but a voice made me jump straight up. A little squeal leaped from my throat before I could stop it.

"Are you ready for breakfast, ma'am?" Mrs. Widlow.

"N-no," I said, my heart hammering in my chest. "I mean... Thank you. Is Mr. Reynolds at breakfast?"

Her stern face didn't even acknowledge my fright. Her grey hair was coiffed in its usual helmet, and today she wore olive green. "Mr. Reynolds has already left for the office."

"Of course," I said, pushing my long dark curls back. "It's ten."

I could breathe easily. And I'd be gone before he even returned home. Even better, his personal computer would be sitting in his office unguarded.

"I am hungry," I said quickly. "Would you please see if I could get eggs benedict?" I hoped a complicated breakfast order would buy me some time.

"Of course," the woman said, turning on her heel.

I watched her walk away a moment before quietly dashing down the main stairs and sneaking to the small room behind them at the bottom.

* * *

The door to Sloan's private office was unlocked, and I hurried around his large desk, opening his notebook computer. The chances of him leaving anything where I might find it were slim to none. He would expect me to search—especially after last night. He would anticipate me going through his things, trying to find out what he was doing. Still, I opened his inbox, quickly scrolling through all the messages, looking for anything, any kind of lead.

Nothing seemed suspicious. It was all travel arrangements, appointments, luncheons, and follow up messages. My heart beat painfully hard. I was running out of time. Mrs. Widlow would be looking for me for breakfast, and this might be my only chance to access this room alone before Elaine arrived. Not only that, I had to make sure I had everything I needed before Elaine did appear. I was never returning to this house again once I left it.

I sat and stared at the computer several minutes trying to think like my soon-to-be ex-husband. He probably had it all on his phone. My shoulders dropped in defeat. But wait! I realized if it was on his smart phone, there ought to be a corresponding email address. And it was possible it might be an online mail provider...

Opening his browser again, I went to the history file and looked for recent mail programs. Hal had picked me up at the airport, so whoever he'd used had been tracking me as recently as that date. I found a link to an Internet mail site and clicked on it, opening a window filled with messages.

My throat closed when I saw the list of names, the numbers, the dates. It was all here—the escort services, the hotel rooms, all over the country... All of it.

For a moment, I only stared stupidly as the tears flooded my eyes. The enormity of his betrayal left me weak and wounded. There were so many.

How had I been so trusting? How had I been such a fool? Years of lies, and I'd never suspected.

With a deep breath, I touched my tears away. This was my past. I didn't have to carry this with me, and Derek had shown me love was waiting in my future. Taking another cleansing breath, I realized this was also a gift in disguise. It was the insurance I needed, the backup that transformed what happened from being his word against mine into cold, hard facts. Now I had evidence.

I slid the mouse and clicked the printer icon. Twenty verified transactions later, I didn't want to know any more. It was enough. With these and the other items in my possession, I was sure my case was solid. I had enough to make my soon-to-be ex-husband cooperate. Now all I needed was the name of Sloan's helper. Whoever it was would have to be moved by the physical evidence of my husband's abuse and betrayal. And if he wasn't, well, maybe it didn't even matter anymore.

I was still scrolling when my eyes landed on the name, and I felt all the blood drain from my face. My hand slid from the mouse, taking my strength with it. I couldn't breathe.

There it was, the name of the person tracking me for my husband, *DAlexander@AlexanderKnight.com*

Chapter 14 – Off the Record

My vibrating phone roused me. I'd sat with my forehead on Sloan's desk for minutes that felt like hours. In one line of text, all the life had gone from my body. My warm light was snuffed out.

I should be crying. The little flicker of hope I'd held so dearly all these days had been cruelly extinguished, and I was left shivering in the cold darkness alone. My entire body braced for the breakdown, but it never came. Only quiet sadness held me unable to move.

The vibrating started again, and finally I lifted my hand to check it. Elaine's face and number blinked at me, but I only stared at her. I couldn't seem to care. I wanted to slide under the desk and stay there forever. Still, my friend persisted.

And even with all the hope sucked out of my life, I knew if she were here, she'd say all the right things. I had to get up. I had to get out of this place and go to the new life I'd been working so hard to establish. Once I was there, I could break down, but not while I was still in this place of danger.

Before I left, however, something in me wanted this last bit of evidence, this last piece of betrayal. I moved the mouse over the print icon and clicked, waiting as the email printed out, not even reading it.

I left Sloan's office quieter and far slower than when I'd entered. I walked down the passage and climbed the stairs to my room before I pressed the button to call my best friend back.

"Melissa!" Elaine's voice was frantic when she answered. "I've been so worried. I couldn't even sleep."

"Where are you?" I managed to ask through the thickness in my throat.

"I'm minutes away. Are you ready?"

Relief washed over me in a wave so powerful, I had to sit on my bed. "Yes, I'm ready. I'm ready now." I felt the breakdown threatening, but I had to be strong. "Oh, Elaine. Thank you so much."

"Oh, honey," she cried. "I'd be there even faster if I could."

I ended the call and pulled myself up by force of will. I had to collect the last of my things. I had to make sure I wasn't leaving behind anything I couldn't live without. I was never looking back.

Opening my closet, I dug through the remaining shoeboxes and old photo albums. The good news was most everything I cared about was in Wilmington now, and as depressing as it sounded, there was very little I wanted to keep from these days in Baltimore. I was just zipping up the large suitcase when I heard the light knock on my door. Looking up, I saw Sloan standing there, a severe line between his light-brown eyebrows.

"What's going on?" he demanded.

I jumped back from the suitcase as if electrocuted. "Why are you here? You're supposed to be at your office."

"Gladys said you were acting strangely, and I should come home."

"Mrs. Widlow," I breathed. As if a switch inside me was flipped, the whole idea that every single person in this house watched me like a rebellious teenager and reported back to Sloan set me off.

The depression I'd been feeling over Derek turned into rage, and I jerked the suitcase off my bed. "There's nothing strange going on," I said, stalking over to my dresser and jerking open the small top drawer. I grasped the pepper spray canister, aiming it straight at his face. "I'm leaving this place. And if you try to stop me, I'll spray you."

Sloan's eyebrow cocked, and he held both hands up as if I'd just pulled a gun. "By all means, leave," he breathed a short laugh. It only fueled my rage.

"Don't test me, Sloan. There's nothing I'd love more than to burn your eyes out."

At that he dropped his hands and walked out. "Have a safe drive," he called over his shoulder.

Just then, Elaine jogged up the main stairway. When she and Sloan met each other, they both stopped. For a moment, I wasn't sure what might happen. My best friend looked at my almost ex-husband as if he were Osama bin Laden, and he looked at her as if she were a witch.

I jerked up the handle on my suitcase and stalked down the hall, rolling it behind me. "I'm here, Elaine!" I called. "Don't bother with him. It's time to go."

Her brow softened, and she turned from Sloan to me. "Let's go," she repeated.

On my way out, my eyes landed on a stack of envelopes sitting on the small table by the front door. The mail! I paused only briefly to spread them out, and my breath caught when I saw it—Aunt Bea's check! It came! I nearly burst into tears at the sight of it. The envelope restored the tiniest bit of hope I needed. I was going to survive this. I was going to be okay. I might be alone, but I was going to make it through.

I snatched it up and walked out the door not looking back. I would never look back.

* * *

We lifted my huge suitcase into Elaine's car and jumped inside. I watched as she guided us out of the long driveway away from the Reynolds mansion, but when we reached the main road, I put my hand on her arm.

"Wait before we get going." My chest ached with what I was about to ask my best friend, but I didn't have a choice. I had to have closure. "There's something I need to do first. Will you help me?"

Her brows drew together, but she waited. "Of course, what is it?"

I pulled out the three pages that included Derek's email and Sloan's response. "I printed this off Sloan's computer. Would you read it to me?"

Elaine was still frowning, but she took the sheets from me. "To DAlexander@AlexanderKnight.com..." Instantly she lowered the pages and looked at me. "Is this... Derek?"

"Please just read it," I said, every muscle in my body clenched.

"Derek, I hope you remember your old mentor Sloan." She stopped again, taking a breath and staring at me, brows clutched.

"Keep going," I whispered.

"I found you online, and I hope you might be willing to do a favor for an old friend. Of course, I'll pay you well." Again she stopped. "Oh, Mel. I don't think I can —"

"Please, Elaine." My voice was sharp now. "Just read the damn email."

She took a deep breath and continued. "I'm afraid my wife is having an affair, and I need someone I can trust to verify this for me. Attached is her photograph and information. She is somewhere this week. She wouldn't tell me where. I think it might be with him."

A knot tightened in my throat, and again Elaine paused. But instead of speaking, she took another deep breath and continued. "As you can imagine, this is very sensitive and quite humiliating. I hope we can keep this off the record."

My head dropped at the phrase. It was the same thing he'd said to me after Patrick had revealed the location of their offices. *Off the record.*

"Your friend, Sloan Reynolds," she finished. Then she lowered the pages to her lap.

His friend. I couldn't speak. I had gone numb and nothing felt like it made sense anymore.

"He was spying on you?" Her voice cracked high with disbelief. "Was Patrick in on it, too?"

I shrugged, blinking slowly. Then I forced the words. "He responded. I printed out the whole exchange."

She lifted the pages again and folded the first one back. "Dear Sloan," then she glanced at me, but I was still sitting frozen, unable to feel. "I'm sorry to hear of your marital difficulties. I did observe your wife this week. She was with another female at the Cactus Flower Spa in Scottsdale, Arizona. But I have to confess, I did not observe her with any male guests. As far as I could tell, she was alone the entire week. Sorry not to be more help. No payment needed. Cordially, Derek."

At that she stared at the printout, her brow lined. She flipped the pages back and forth, then she turned to me in her seat. "Weren't you and Derek...?"

For a moment, all I could do was stare at my lap in stunned silence. Then I slowly nodded, finding my voice. "We were together," I said softly.

Her eyebrows flew up. "You *slept* together?"

"Several times."

"But he said..." She looked out the front window a moment. "I don't understand."

I reached for the door handle, lifting it, and getting out of the car. I went around and opened the hatchback, unzipping my suitcase and digging through the file folders I'd placed on top until I found the one I was looking for. I walked back to the passenger's side and got in, pulling the door closed. Then I reached down by my feet and dug out the small silk pouch I'd hidden in my bag.

"Would you please do something for me, Elaine?" I looked at my friend with such seriousness, she immediately nodded. "I need you to drive us to Princeton. There's something I have to do."

Her jaw dropped. "But—"

"Please? Sloan can't call the shots any more."

I watched as she chewed her lip. Then she grasped the steering wheel and turned her car toward Interstate 95.

CHAPTER 15 – THE HUMILIATING TRUTH

The Alexander-Knight office was easy to find using the directions on my smart phone, and we were pulling into the corporate entrance in less than two hours. Neither Elaine nor I had spoken much on the drive over. She had turned on talk radio shortly after leaving Baltimore and withdrawn into her own private thoughts. I could only assume she was processing like me, and I welcomed her silence. I wasn't sure how well she was keeping up with Patrick since our trip to Scottsdale, but I was almost certain he hadn't told her about this.

As for me, I was still reeling from my discovery, and I'd spent the entire time thinking and re-thinking what I planned to say. Derek had lied to me, slept with me, known the entire time I was dealing with a pending divorce and a suspicious husband, and he'd never said a word.

Sloan called him his friend. The very thought of them being friends made me sick and angry and nauseated and... miserable. I wanted to believe Derek didn't know the extent of Sloan's atrocities, still if he thought of himself as a hero, a gallant fellow who'd protected my honor, I wanted to be sure he knew the full extent of how he had helped his "friend."

Elaine pulled into the front parking lot and sat in the car looking up at the building. The exterior looked exactly as it did on the company website — limestone and blonde brick, silver windows, four floors. It was one of several office buildings clustered in a pentagon formation and sharing a common entrance and courtyard. In keeping with the season, it was decorated in orange, black, and purple, corn stalks and autumn wreaths. Someone had hung what appeared to be a witch smashing into the trunk of one of the trees. Stuffed arms and legs were splayed on either side of it along with a wrecked broomstick. I was sure it was meant to be funny, but nothing in me felt like laughing.

"I don't think I can go in there," Elaine whispered. "I can't see Patrick right now. I still haven't decided what I want to say to him."

"Well, I know exactly what I want to say." I grasped the door handle and stepped out of the car. "Wait here. I won't be long."

I had the two manila folders in my hands and the small silk pouch. What I intended to do would take less than fifteen minutes.

Stepping into the lobby of Office Building A, I scanned the directory until I located them on the fourth floor. The only thing I hadn't considered was they might be out to lunch, but I wasn't letting anything slow me down. I was acting on pure adrenaline now.

The elevator opened to a sleek, glass and stainless suite. Their entrance had the names Alexander & Knight lasered into the glass doors, and a receptionist's desk was situated right in the center of an open foyer with white leather chairs placed near a low, mahogany table.

Copies of *Forbes*, *Time*, and oddly an *OK!* magazine were arranged on the table. I stalked out, headed straight for his door. The blonde receptionist said something I ignored. I scanned the plaques outside each until I found the one reading *Derek Alexander*. I didn't even knock before entering his huge, corner office. He was turned in his black leather desk chair looking out a wall of windows, but when he heard the door, he started speaking.

"I don't know how you do it, Patrick," he breathed, turning the chair around as he finished. "I can't stop thinking..." His eyes locked on mine. "About her."

Derek stood quickly, and seeing him again for the first time since that week, dressed in grey slacks and a dress shirt unbuttoned at the top, blue eyes glowing beneath his dark brow, I had to fight all the emotions warring in my chest. The physical longing, the anger, the betrayal, the unbelievable, gut-wrenching pain. I ignored all of it—including the weakness in my knees at the blaze in his eyes when he saw me. I forced my mind to focus on what he'd done.

"Melissa," he said. "What—" He started around the desk toward me when I cut him off.

"Don't come any closer," I said. My stomach was in knots, and seeing the expression on his face—the frown melting into joy going back to a frown at my words—it took everything I had to control myself, to take it slow and be a professional. To handle him the way he'd handled me.

He stopped. "I don't understand. I'm so happy to see you. I-I want to—"

"Just hold that thought," I said, my hand extended as I walked to the opposite side of the desk from him. "I'm here for a reason."

"To see me, I hope," his voice was soft and low. It made my eyes burn.

My jaw clenched against any display of emotion. I'd had enough of men and their games. "It seems you know my ex-husband Sloan. You did some work for him a few weeks ago? In Scottsdale?"

Instantly his shoulders dropped. "Oh, Mel," he exhaled. "I can explain—" he started toward me again, palms out.

"Not until I've said what I came here to say."

His hands dropped and he studied my face. Then he nodded as if he understood, but I was pretty sure he didn't. "Will you sit?" he asked, going back around to his chair.

"I won't be that long." I pulled out one of the manila folders I'd brought, opening it on his desk and taking out the first document—the printout of their email exchange. "You confirmed for him that I was at the spa resort, but you saw no signs of me with a man? I suppose that was to cover your ass."

"No," he started. "It wasn't. I wanted to let you decide what you wanted—"

"Save it to the end," I continued, pulling out the next sheet. "I guess he told you his side of the story. That he didn't know why I was trying to leave him, that I must have another man somewhere. Maybe that I was crazy? I know he repeatedly told the staff such lies, and he always wondered aloud how I could throw away our life together."

Derek's lips pressed into a line, but he didn't speak. He waited for me to finish.

The next print out was a copy of the confirmation from the first escort service. "He wasn't so worried about our life together when he started fucking prostitutes."

I pulled out another contact, then another. One by one, I put the sheets on his desk, and Derek lifted them. I watched the muscle in his jaw flex as he quickly scanned their contents.

"The first time he said it was the long trip," I continued. "He was missing me, horny as hell, I think he said. And with a prostitute, it didn't count, right? She was just a faceless whore."

His eyes traveled back to me, but I could tell he was waiting, letting me say what I needed to say.

"After that, I couldn't sleep with him anymore." My voice wavered a bit. It was the first time I was saying all of this out loud. And to the one person I had mistakenly thought I could trust.

"That was about a year ago, right after we moved to Baltimore. Six months ago, he decided he was tired of waiting for me to get over it. Marriage counseling wasn't working, and he wanted to fuck his wife, goddammit."

At that, I pulled out the photo I'd guarded so closely. The one I'd never wanted anyone to see. The humiliating truth I still couldn't get my mind around. It had happened to me. *To me!* And I'd always believed I was smarter than that, a better judge of character. Seemed I was wrong twice.

I paused, studying the glossy print a moment, my throat tightening. Then I placed it in front of Derek, shame radiating through my chest.

"Of course, I fought him." The thickness in my voice made it difficult to speak. "And he fought back."

Derek only glanced at the photo before his eyes closed, his hand formed a fist on his desk. The picture showed my battered face. My lips swollen and purple, my black eyes, the cut at my hairline that really should've gotten stitches. It didn't show the bruises covering my torso.

I only had this picture because I'd called Elaine in hysterics. She'd dropped everything and drove all night, six hours to find me in the hotel room. She'd insisted, no, demanded I go to the police. She wanted to call her dad, her brother, every male we knew to beat the shit out of him. But I wouldn't. I didn't want anyone to know what had happened to me.

So she'd insisted I let her take pictures. "For when you come to your senses," she'd said, "and want him dead."

It was the one bit of evidence I'd held onto in case the asshole, bastard, son-of-a-bitch loser I was living with decided he wouldn't let me go.

"The next day," I continued speaking to Derek. "When he saw what he'd done, he laughed and said something about how it wasn't so long ago, raping your wife wasn't even considered a crime."

Derek stood quickly then, eyes blazing. "Melissa, you have to believe me. I didn't know about this. I never wanted—"

"To hurt me? To fuck with me? Well, I guess you did fuck with me. Several times." I walked to the window and looked out. "That's the part I don't understand. Why did you do that? Was it a little something extra for you? Tap the wayward wife?"

I heard him exhale deeply. "I told you why," he said, jaw clenched. "I cared about you. I wanted to be with you. I still do."

"Were you even there for the conference?"

His lips tightened, and I realized the answer. The conference was just a lucky coincidence. A convenient lie.

I shook my head. "Thanks, but no thanks. You're no hero. You're a liar. And if you were trying to hurt me you couldn't have done a better job."

I stepped back to his desk, turning the photograph facedown and sliding it and the other papers together and into the folders, preparing to leave. But then I remembered. I turned back and placed the silk pouch on the smooth desk's surface. In it was the necklace with the floating heart he'd given me in Scottsdale.

"I almost threw this into the ocean," I said, holding my voice steady. "But that didn't seem harsh enough. Now I simply don't want it anymore. Or you."

His eyes were pleading as he tried to approach me again, but I stepped back, clutching the folder to my chest. My voice shook as I said my final words, and I was afraid I'd over-stayed my ability not to cry. "Don't ever come near me again."

I went straight out and closed his office door, pausing for a moment to lean against it. I exhaled a trembling breath, closing my eyes, but when I heard him approaching on the other side, I quickly walked to the main entrance and dashed out, taking the stairs down instead of waiting for the elevator.

It was over. Nothing he could say could make it right. He'd lied to me. The entire time we were together in Arizona had been a lie. He'd known every time he'd slept with me why he was there, why I was there, and he'd never said a word. I could never trust him again.

All I wanted was to get as far away from him as possible—from all of this. I wanted to go back to

Wilmington, back to my old life, and never, never remember my time in Maryland. Ever again.

CHAPTER 16 – THE ROAD TO ANYWHERE

Sitting on the shore outside my new home, I watched the sun set as the tide gently rolled in against my feet. In the three months since I'd been back, it felt like I had almost completely regained my life. Yes, there were a few scars, a few old wounds, but I was healing. Now I could actually see a time when I'd be whole, unlike before when I was only sinking further into despair.

My old friends were waiting with open arms. Of course, all of them except Elaine got the modified version of why I'd left Sloan. The most I was comfortable revealing was that he'd had an affair. And while there were a few people who didn't understand why I couldn't just forgive him and put it behind us, more people seemed to support me.

Restarting my marketing business proved easier than I'd anticipated. I'd been afraid my old clients had moved on or forgotten about me, but they hadn't. Taking over Mrs. Reynolds' positions on the Baltimore boards had been more beneficial than I'd realized at the time, and now that I was off my "sabbatical," as I framed it, many of them referred new clients to me. In less than a month, I was adding to the spreadsheet of names I'd started that night in my old room in Sloan's mansion.

Only one name had been removed, and I was doing my best to forget it.

I hadn't asked Derek what to do about his childhood game, when the thing you were holding onto for survival was taken away. I supposed the answer would be to simply survive. To keep going. Push through the pain and carry on. Wait for the day when it no longer hurt. He said the pain always ended. I had to believe in this one thing at least, he was telling the truth.

That entire drive back from Princeton, I'd held on with all my might. Seeing him again for the first time that way, after longing for him so hard had been like a million kicks to the chest and stomach. But knowing what he'd done, how he'd deceived me, only twisted all that pain even tighter into a bitter knot.

When I'd finally gotten my keys from the realtor and signed the papers on my new home, I'd thanked my best friend, who had to get back to her work at school, and I'd allowed myself to cry for a long time.

The delay in moving back to Wilmington had given me time to have all my services connected and everything set up from Maryland. My one-bedroom, single bath condo was small, but it was gorgeous, designed for the discriminating beachcomber. The floor-plan was open and airy. It had a gourmet kitchen—

complete with brushed stainless appliances and fixtures — a dining area, and a study with a window seat. I even had a private, screened-in porch.

The color scheme was all white and the floors were bright pine, but I'd already decided I'd add color to the interior. Not immediately, as my heart felt like all the color had been drained away. But everything was ready to go as soon as I was ready to pull myself out of the bed.

It was a battle. It took longer than I cared to admit, but I'd gotten back on my feet, and now we were headed into the holiday season.

My only setback occurred a month after I arrived. Halloween had passed, and I was doing my best to rebuild my client base. Elaine recommended I visit the private school where she worked to leave a card. I hadn't made it over until the end of the day, and walking from the parking lot, I couldn't help noticing a well-dressed, well-built, honey-blond male walking near me. I jumped two feet when I realized who it was.

"Patrick!" I breathed as his hazel eyes lit with recognition.

"Hello, Melissa." That handsome smile crossed his lips, and I felt like an idiot. I should've known they were still together.

Just as fast, I grew tense. "Are you alone? Is — "

"I'm alone," he said. "Had some business in Raleigh, so I figured I'd drop in on my way back. Surprise Elaine."

"This isn't on your way back."

"It can be."

My lips pressed together. Elaine had been kind enough never to mention what happened in Princeton or the guys at all since my return to Wilmington. At the same time, Brian was ancient history, and she never dated anyone to my knowledge, which was very unusual for my flirtatious friend. Now it all made sense.

"I'm sorry," I blinked down, studying my tan pumps. "I hadn't realized you two were still together. Elaine doesn't talk about it."

"I know." We were standing in the parking lot, and he crossed his toned arms over his equally toned chest. "We thought it would be easier if we gave you two some space for now."

"For now?" I shook my head. "You can be as open as you like. Derek and I are through."

His lips parted then closed, and I could tell he was trying to decide what to say. "I'd like to be a little more open with you. If you'll hear me out."

"Patrick, please..."

"I don't want to offend you or pick at a fresh wound," his voice turned gentle, "but if you're still deciding—"

"I've already decided..." Sadness burned in my throat stronger than the anger I normally used to fight it.

Seeing Patrick reminded me too much of being with Derek, of being held in those strong arms, of that deep sense of safety he'd given me. He had been so comforting after my year of nightmares. Of course, I'd fallen in love with him. I was an idiot.

"Derek's wife died six years ago," Patrick continued. "He wasn't the same for a long time. Not until..."

My eyes burned with rapidly forming tears. "Please stop," I whispered.

"He had no idea, Mel. Neither of us knew what you'd been through."

"He should've told me the truth," I said. Two tears splashed onto my cheeks when I blinked, and I angrily wiped them away. "He lied to me. That's all that matters."

"He's sorry."

I spun on my heel and headed back to my car. The last thing I needed was to hear about his regret. Any man who could do what he did, get as close to me as he did, and then lie, hide something that important, was capable of anything. And I'd already been down the road to anything. I wasn't revisiting the location.

Derek Alexander was a thing of my past, and if I never met another man as long as I lived, I'd be happy.

* * *

My beach condo was absolutely perfect for my recovery. Just being in it made me feel peace. It also made me feel lucky, like I was getting another chance.

It was part of what had been envisioned as a planned beach community near Sea Breeze that fell victim to the recession. When the developers went broke, they sold off what was left for cheap, and I happened to be on the market at the exact right moment. It was as if all the negatives in my life had managed to twist out one beautiful positive for me.

Since the location was only partially developed, I was secluded from much of the tourist traffic that regularly invaded the area. Most of my neighbors were full-time residents who'd lucked into their properties as well. We were all bound together by sandy paths and picket fences, and we valued the seclusion of our area. Our dunes were untrodden, and the sea oats and beach scrub formed a nice barrier between us and the high-end resorts nearby.

Sitting on the shore, I inhaled the salty air, tasting it on my tongue. I straightened my shoulders and allowed the warmth of gratitude to tingle through every part of my body. I was alone, but I was content in this new, healing chapter of my life.

Except when Elaine visited. Since I'd bumped into Patrick that day, she'd stopped tip-toeing around their relationship. And my former one.

"Patrick said he does nothing but monitor Sloan now," she said, removing the ingredients for our dinner from the brown bag she'd brought with her. I was busy opening a bottle of wine. "He's determined to catch him breaking the law and bring him down."

"I don't care, Elaine," I said in my usual monotone when she got on this subject. "And I'm so tired of having this conversation. Derek and I are through."

"But he's still in love with you," she insisted. "And he wants that bastard to pay."

"And you're a hopeless romantic," I said, pouring us both large globes of red wine. "I'm a little irritated you didn't tell me you were still dating Patrick. He was in on the lie, too, you know."

"He didn't know you were sleeping with Derek," she said. "You didn't even tell me that part until after!"

"You couldn't see anything but each other," I said taking a sip. "Besides, he knew they were there to spy on us, and he didn't tell you. How can that not drive you crazy?"

"Mmm... Patrick drives me crazy in other ways." She winked, taking a sip of her wine.

I rolled my eyes. "You're impossible."

"And I think you're secretly in love with Derek."

"I'm not talking about this with you anymore." She couldn't understand because she'd never been hurt like I had. "I won't be with someone who could lie to me like that. So convincingly."

"Patrick said he wanted to stay out of it and let you decide what to do about your marriage. He was hoping you'd come to him once it was over—if it was over."

I shook my head, my voice growing thick. "When the man you love, the man you married, attempts to rape you, then beats you when you try to defend yourself, it makes it impossible to tolerate much from anyone. Ever again."

"Oh, Mel," Elaine crossed the kitchen to me, tears in her eyes. "We don't have to talk about it anymore." She pulled me into a hug, and I held her waist. For a moment we were both silent, remembering that horrible night, how it changed everything. Including me.

"I just care about you," she said, wiping her nose. "And I know Derek's sorry. He's such a good guy."

"Let's have some dinner," I said, going to the bag. I pulled out the box of ziti while she began cutting a pepper.

"Patrick wants to relocate," she said quietly, sliding the ingredients into the waiting sauté pan. "Since their work is primarily online, he'd like to move here."

My lips pressed together as I filled a pot with water and put it on the stove to boil the pasta. Once it was going, I picked up my glass again and leaned against the counter. "Are you two that serious?"

She shrugged. "Maybe. I mean, it's hard to know when we're separated. Distance makes everything so emotionally charged. It's like the first time every time."

"Sounds like you two are enjoying some hot reunions."

Elaine blushed then laughed. "It almost makes me want to maintain the distance."

The water was boiling, and I turned to dump in the ziti. For a few moments, I watched it, poking the dry noodles with a wooden spoon. My mind drifted to the time I'd had with Derek. Had our intensity all been a product of some feeling of urgency?

He had known the whole time I was married, but he claimed he didn't know how bad my situation was. Was he afraid I wouldn't leave Sloan? Did he think I might decide to stay with my husband?

I shook my head. It didn't matter.

"So the marketing business is booming?" My friend was finished chopping and handed off the raw ingredients to me before hopping up on the counter.

I took her handiwork and pushed it all into the pan, cranking up the heat and stirring rapidly. "It is, and thanks to you, Saint Samuel's has become one of my most loyal clients."

"Good. They need the help." Her little school was trying to grow but struggling against new, free charter options. "Have you heard any more from... him?"

I sighed and turned the heat down to let everything simmer. "Sloan tried giving me trouble over the divorce proceedings, but I faxed those emails to Thomas. He said I'd have my final paperwork by the end of next week."

"He's such a prick," Elaine growled, taking a sip of her wine. "I still can't believe you didn't take him for everything he has."

"I don't want anything he has," I said, sipping my own wine. "He's a bastard fucknut, and I hope I never see him again."

"A no-nut sphincter taster."

I snorted and caught my nose with my hand. "A what?!" I cried.

Elaine split into laughter. "I don't know. It's something my brother used to say."

"Come on," I pulled her off the counter. "Let's go eat."

Elaine stayed until after midnight. We enjoyed the spicy ziti and peppers with our red wine and finished it all off with coffee and tiramisu. I asked her to spend the night, but she insisted she had to get up early for a teacher's meeting the next day. So we hugged each other, and she started back for the mainland.

After she left, I walked down to the shore again—this time using my flashlight. It was a secluded area, and that only increased my risk of getting lost in the dark. But I was careful, and I was learning my way around my new landscape.

At the water's edge, I sat and reconsidered everything Elaine and Patrick had told me. I thought about Derek losing his wife, and the pain he must have felt to spend six years alone. What about me had brought him out of that isolation? Did he connect to a shared sense of loss? Was I able to help him find his way back from that sadness? Could he help me?

I thought about getting away from Sloan. Once the final divorce papers were in, I'd be free and I could truly recover from the disappointment and ultimately the trauma that had been my married life. After that, I could think about maybe talking to people and perhaps giving certain people second chances. If those people were still interested.

Who knew, perhaps it was possible the road to anywhere could turn into a road to somewhere. For both of us.

Chapter 17 – Finally Over

My mother was visiting the day my divorce papers arrived. We both sat at the kitchen table drinking coffee when the postman rang the bell. He carried a package wrapped in brown paper and a long, legal-sized envelope along with assorted letters and bills. I handed Mom the package to open as I pulled the brown envelope apart. She let out an exclamation of delight, but my face fell. In her hands was a box of cupcakes from Bea's Fancy Cakes, but in mine were several long, legal-sized sheets. At the very top of the first page, in bold, all-capital letters were the words **FINAL DECREE**.

Despite everything that had happened, all the pain and humiliation, a sick lump of failure tightened in the back of my throat. I swallowed it down and blinked to her frowning eyes. She slowly lowered her happy gift.

"Oh, Mel. How are you doing really?" she asked in her best psychiatrist's voice.

"I'm relieved, of course," I exhaled, trying to smile. "But I confess, seeing my name there in black and white followed by DIVORCE in all caps..." I shrugged. "I can't help remembering how optimistic I was on our wedding day. I thought my life would be so different."

To her credit, my mother only nodded. Once I'd returned to Wilmington, she'd dropped all suggestions that I try to work things out with Sloan. She immediately switched to supportive mode, and any indications that I might have made a mistake were gone. I assumed she reserved those types of urgings for the pre-divorce discussions, and now that it was over, so were they. Either way, I was thankful. Yet at the same time, I could sense she knew there was more I wasn't telling her.

"Here," she said, putting the package on the counter and going to my refrigerator. She opened the door and pulled out a bottle of champagne I'd stuck in the back — in case of celebration. I'd read a quote that said sometimes just having a bottle of champagne in the fridge could be a reason to celebrate. That was two months ago.

"It's time to open this guy," she said.

"What?" My brows pulled together in disbelief.

"We're celebrating. It's a new chapter in your life." I watched as she twisted the wire basket off the cork and then popped it.

"Talk about pendulum swings."

Mom shook her head. "You were very different when you got back home three months ago. I didn't say anything at the time, but you had a definite look in your eyes."

I pulled two flutes down from the cabinet and placed them in front of her to fill.

"Was it the look of a crazy person?"

"We don't use that term in the profession," she gently scolded as she poured. We waited for the fizz to settle, then she held my glass out. "You looked like you'd been through a long and difficult battle."

I took the sparkling wine from her. "I had," I said softly.

"You looked nearly broken," her voice strained. "It hurt so much to see the remnants of that kind of pain on your face."

My mom's eyes were brown, but she had my dark curls. Our eyes met in a warm understanding, and she stepped forward. "I believe you did the right thing," she said, pulling me into a hug. "I'm sorry I ever questioned you."

For a moment, I relaxed in her healing embrace. She didn't know the full story; I didn't want her to know the full story. It was enough that we were here. It was more than enough. My head rested on her shoulder, and I held her waist.

A few minutes passed and I stepped back, giving her a smile. I sniffed and wiped my eyes. "Thanks, Mom."

Then she clinked her glass to mine. "Here's to a better future."

I smiled and agreed, taking a sip.

* * *

Mom stayed through dinner, and we had one of our best visits since I'd married Sloan. It was a cold night, and she pulled on one of my sweaters. I lit the gas log, and we sat close together in front of the fireplace sipping coffee and eating the luscious cinnamon-bun cupcakes.

They were warm and comforting and perfectly timed, considering what else arrived with them. Not only that, they were cupcakes like only Aunt Bea could make—moist and buttery cake with a slightly spicy cinnamon ribbon swirling through the middle. On top was a deliciously crusty buttercrème frosting that was the exact flavor of cinnamon bun icing. We were both swooning from the first bite.

"None of my clients send me gifts like this," Mom teased, finishing her small confection.

"Isn't Bea the best?" I agreed, taking another nibble. "She can't figure out the Internet, but I convinced her I could maintain her account from here. And I still get my seasonal treats."

Mom placed her hand over mine and rubbed. "I'm glad to hear Baltimore wasn't all bad."

I nodded. "There are great people there. Bea was one of the best."

Aunt Bea might not understand how small the world had become, but she did know how to show kindness from any distance. Her gifts went a long way toward restoring my faith in both humanity and in one's ability to recover from any setback.

"I need a tree," I said, taking a sip of coffee and hoping to transition the conversation away from the past. Christmas was coming, and Mom loved decorating.

It was the perfect detour, and she immediately launched into the different options I might choose. That led to the topic of gifts, so I pulled out my Macbook. We spent the next few hours looking at pin boards and making lists, until she announced it was late.

I walked her out, promising to drive in and spend the night with her the next weekend—we could complete our lists, do some shopping. For a few moments I stood outside in the cold air, listening to the waves crashing far off and watching the taillights of her car fade into the distance.

Slowly I went back inside and put our dishes in the dishwasher. Our champagne flutes were still in front of the fireplace, but I was tired. I walked to my bedroom ready to wash my face and slip between the cool sheets. Halfway there, I heard a noise in the kitchen. A banging as if a window were falling.

"Mom?" I called, swiftly going back down the hall. "Did you forget something?"

The scream was out of my mouth before a thought registered in my brain. Sloan stood in the kitchen doorway, backlit by the yellow lights. "It's only me, hon."

I dashed into the living room and ran around the couch, putting as much space between us as possible. Quickly, I scanned my room for anything to use as a weapon. All I saw was a lamp.

"S-Sloan..." I caught my breath, struggling to keep my voice calm, not fearful. Authoritative and not yielding my ground. "What are you doing here?"

"That's not very a welcoming remark," he said, with a grin, a wicked glint in his eye. "We're supposed to show guests that southern hospitality, aren't we?"

"What do you want?" I reached for the lamp, resting my hand on the neck and waiting.

"Nice place," he said, surveying my new home. "I see you got your divorce papers today. Not celebrating, I hope."

Fear stole the air from my lungs as he quickly crossed the room to me. I snatched up the lamp, but he caught my wrist, jerking it and sending the fixture crashing to the floor. I tried to pull my arm away, but he held it fast, turning me so my back was pressed firmly against his chest.

"You bet I'm celebrating," I grunted, struggling to free myself from his grip. "My time with you is over. Legally. And forever."

He only held me closer, wrapping my other arm around my waist and holding me still. "And what are you telling all your old friends about our divorce? That I slept with prostitutes? That I beat you?"

I shivered with dread as his breath whooshed across the back of my neck. "No," I said, fighting to keep my voice calm, to stay in control. "I figured that was too much information."

He laughed. "I'll say. Especially since it was all your fault."

I struggled so hard to get away from him, my shoulders ached. Finally I gave up. I'd have to out-think him. I wasn't strong enough to overpower him. For starters, I wouldn't fall for his tricks. He knew as well as I did what happened that night. And whose fault it was.

"You still haven't told me why you're here," I said. "What do you want?"

His voice was right at my ear. "I want you, of course. You're incredibly sexy as a single woman. And we never said a proper goodbye."

His grip loosened on my arms, and I jerked them both free. He only caught me by the waist and pulled me back. "I hope you're not planning to fight me again. You know I'll win."

My stomach lurched, and I hated the dread his words triggered in me. I had to calm my mind, I had to think. Somehow, I had to throw him off and then make my escape.

Taking a deep breath, and closing my eyes for a moment, I relaxed my fighting. I imagined getting a gift on Christmas morning, happy feelings. I tried to make my voice sound like I was having a pleasant realization.

"You're saying you want to spend the night here?" I was all innocence now. "I guess that's a good idea. You're pretty far from Baltimore, and it's very late."

The smile returned to his voice and he released me. "To be clear, my dear, I'm not just looking to spend the night. I'm looking to fuck somebody. Namely you. I vaguely recall you're not too bad in the sack."

I swallowed the tightness in my throat and turned to face him. "But I don't understand. Why me? Why not call an escort service?" My eyes flickering around the room, double-checking for something to hit him with. "You know you prefer them." The words were bitter on my tongue, but I was playing a part, buying time.

"Thanks for your concern about my satisfaction," he said, lifting an empty champagne flute and sniffing it. "But I confess, my interest in you is renewed now that you've added an 'ex' to your prefix. You're still a hot little piece of ass. Oh, and I wanted to let you know, I'm aware you've got someone keeping tabs on me."

My mind was still working, trying to figure out an escape plan, but that made me pause. "I don't have anyone watching you."

"Whatever you say," he breathed, unbuttoning his shirt. "But I'm not an idiot, darling." He pulled the shirt tail out of his pants and started toward me.

I'd given up on finding a weapon. Tomorrow I was buying a bat, but for now, I had to get out of this house. I grabbed my empty flute and headed for the kitchen.

"I'll fix us both a drink. White or red?" My plan at this point was to run for it—even if it was into the dark night, even if it was bitterly cold, and I'd probably end up lost. I'd figure that out once I was away.

"Whatever you're having is fine," he called after me.

My innocent act must have worked. I couldn't believe he let me leave the room, but I hurried into the kitchen, hoping my purse was still sitting on the counter. It wasn't.

I was contemplating my bare feet when a massive arm swept me off the ground by my waist. A hand clamped tight over my mouth to keep me from screaming, and I was held tightly against a solid chest.

"It's me," Derek's voice was barely audible, right beside my ear. "I'm here to help you."

My heart hammered against my ribs as he gently lowered me to my feet again. I was shaking all over as I turned to face him, relief coursing through me.

As always, I noticed how the black tee he wore was stretched tight over his chest, but tonight, my attention was on his biceps straining at the sleeves, his hands clenched in fists. I almost burst into tears at the sight, and just as fast, all I could think was I wanted him to beat the shit out of Sloan.

"Mel?" I heard Sloan's voice from the living room. "You okay in there?"

Derek held a finger over his lips and then circled two fingers around each other as if to indicate "keep it going." He held up a digital recorder, and I bit my lip nodding.

"Yeah," I said, swallowing the knot in my throat. "No clean wine glasses."

"I can help with that," he answered.

"No!" I said quickly. "It's okay. In fact..." I went to the doorway and back into the living room. "I've changed my mind. You're not staying here. In fact, it's time for you to go. Now. I don't want you here anymore."

If Derek was doing what I thought he was, I needed to make this count.

"What?" Sloan said, turning to face me, his expression of surprise turning into anger and thinly veiled arousal. He made me sick. "I thought we'd moved past the rough stuff. But I'm happy to revisit it. Whatever you want."

"I don't want any of your *stuff*," I said, wondering if I should speak louder. "Take your shit and get out of my house. We're not married anymore."

His smile was tight over his gritted teeth, and he crossed the room to me quickly, grabbing my arm and bending it back behind me. "You little bitch," he hissed. "You'll take whatever I give you and like it. As much money as I spent on you."

"Ouch!" I tried to jerk my arm away, but he pulled it higher up my back. "You're hurting me," I said loudly.

I was in real pain, but more importantly, I wanted this on the record. This time, I wanted him to pay.

"Then stop fighting," he said, pulling me against his pelvis by the front of my jeans and flicking my top button loose with his fingers.

"Or what?" My voice was still loud. "You'll rape me? Beat me again?"

"It's not rape if you like it," he said, moving in for a kiss.

"I said no, Sloan!" I said his name loud and clear, bracing to have to fight him, to do whatever it took for Derek to get the evidence he needed.

I was just closing my eyes when I felt the swish of air from a fast-moving body followed by a loud *crack!* My eyes blinked open, and Sloan was on the floor. My piece of shit ex-husband moved once before he passed out completely.

It took me a second to register what had happened. Derek stood over him looking down, breathing hard. His jaw was clenched as were his fists, and it looked like he might do more, like one punch wasn't enough to satisfy him. And while I'd have been happy for him to beat Sloan beyond recognition, I didn't want anything to ruin our chances of putting that loser away.

I quickly stepped in front of Derek, placing my hands on his arms. "I'm okay," I said, pulling him gently. My whole body was trembling. I couldn't seem to stop it, but I had to get him to look at me and not Sloan lying on the floor. "I'm okay, Derek."

As if waking, Derek blinked to me and then took a deep breath. His worried eyes traveled over my face briefly before he leaned down to wrap his arms around my waist, pulling me tight against his body. My insides melted, and tears flooded my eyes. I wasn't sure if it was from the close-call, or post-traumatic stress, or if it was just holding him again this way. Maybe it was a combination of all three, but I gripped my arms around his neck and held him as my body shook with sobs.

"It's okay," he whispered, stroking my hair. "It's over. I will never let him hurt you again."

I nodded against his chest, and he held me several long moments. His hands stroked my back gently until I could finally breathe again without jerking out a sob.

Derek straightened up and lifted my chin with his finger, looking into my eyes. "Okay?" he said, sliding his thumbs gently over my damp cheeks.

I sniffed and nodded, wiping my nose with my hand. "Why were you here?" I asked, as he released me to pull out his phone.

"I never stopped watching him." He was touching the phone quickly as he spoke. "Ever since that day you came to my office, I've been keeping tabs on him."

Elaine had told me that... I stepped away, going to the kitchen to get a tissue and check my face. "But why?" I called back. "Did you have a reason to think he was going to—"

"I had no idea Sloan had turned into such a fucked up loser when he contacted me about you," he said, following me into the kitchen. "But after you showed me that picture..." his lips tightened. "It's a pattern of behavior. I had a feeling he might try it again."

He stepped to the door leading out. "I just need to make a quick call and get somebody out here," he said. "Don't worry, I'll talk to them. I'll keep it out of the media."

His words sent such a wave of relief over me. He'd said the one thing I'd needed to hear, the thing that had held me silent before, without even knowing it.

"Thank you," I whispered.

"You'll still have to answer some questions, but I'll do what I can."

Before he went through the door, I stepped forward and caught his arm, pulling him back. He paused, and I leaned in, pressing a kiss to his cheek. "You are a hero. You're my hero."

His eyes gleamed and he touched my face gently with the back of his index finger. Happiness filled my chest. "I only wish I'd known sooner," he said.

* * *

Police arrived in an unmarked vehicle, and Sloan was handcuffed and taken into custody. I had to make a statement, but Derek stayed beside me. His background was a huge assist in corroborating my story, but the real clincher was the recording he'd made. That combined with the picture I'd shown him from before provided enough evidence to form the basis of a solid case.

"We need to ask a few questions," the officer started, but Derek stopped him.

"I know what you need to know," he said. "Would you let me ask her?"

"We have to hear her answers," the man said.

Derek turned to me sitting at my small table and held both my hands. "There's only a few things they need to know."

I nodded, focusing on his blue eyes.

"Do you want to press charges against Sloan Reynolds?"

"Yes," I said softly. "I didn't before, but I do now."

"In the photo from before, clearly you were beaten." Derek paused and stroked the back of my hands gently. "Did he also rape you that night?"

I shook my head. "He tried, but when I hit him, everything changed. After that he only beat me." My throat grew thick as I remembered Sloan's face as he hit and kicked me. The sick gleam in his eyes. I was afraid I might cry, but I pushed on. "It was as if he got off on beating me."

Derek's lips tightened, and I watched him inhale slowly, the muscle in his jaw flexed. "Would you be willing to share those emails with us? It's possible he also beat one or more of those women. I'd like to track them down and see if any of them will talk. Maybe take a plea deal."

Squeezing his hands, I stood and walked slowly to my bedroom, feeling slightly light-headed. I had planned never to share this information with anyone. I only kept it as insurance, in case I needed it to make Sloan behave or leave me alone. I went to my closet and dug out the two manila folders then returned to the kitchen. Derek and the officer were talking softly, the officer was making notes, but when I appeared they both fell silent.

"Here," I said. "There were more. Many more, but these are the only ones I printed out."

The officer nodded and took the stack from me. Derek stood and squeezed my upper arm gently. "Hang tight. I'll just walk these guys out. See if they have any more questions."

Once they were gone, I walked slowly to my living room, dropping onto the couch. I was exhausted and still a little shaky, but at the same time, I felt hopeful. It was possible this was finally over. This horrible chapter was finally closed.

Chapter 18 - Sharing Everything

Finally, after what seemed like a long time, everyone but Derek was gone. Sloan's car was impounded, and the only noises left at my house were the cicadas and the waves breaking softly in the distance.

"They might want to question Elaine, since she was the only person who saw what happened the first time," he said, standing in my kitchen.

I nodded, blinking up at him, seeing him in a new way tonight. "I can't believe how relieved I feel," I said. "I thought I was through with Sloan. I thought once the divorce was final and I was back here it was over. But I see now I was always fearful. And it would never be over while he was free."

He nodded. "I know." Then he straightened, putting his hands in his back pockets and causing the shirt to stretch over his chest. "I'm sorry, Mel. I'm so sorry for my part in all this. I really had no idea when he emailed me—"

I stood quickly. "Please don't," I said. "After tonight, your apology is so accepted. And maybe... maybe I've started to understand why you didn't tell me."

His brow relaxed, and a glimmer of hope shone in his eyes. He took a small step in my direction. "I swear, when I saw you that night in the bar, all I wanted was to take you from him. I wanted you to be mine." My heart squeezed at his words, and he continued. "I know that makes me a bad person, but you were so gorgeous. And so clearly miserable. I only wanted to make you happy, to see you smile."

"I was unbelievably miserable," I said softly, remembering the first night of that trip. "But you changed all that. And now you've changed it even more."

He took another small step towards me. "I wanted to tell you what was going on so much, but, well, I felt if there was a chance for your marriage, I should step aside and let you work it out. As much as I hated it, he'd found you first."

I breathed a laugh, shaking my head. "You stepped aside after you fucked me like nobody in the world ever had."

He was right in front of me then, and he cautiously reached out to hold my waist. "If it makes any difference, it was a pretty new experience for me, too."

My hands rested on his biceps, and I met his eyes teasing. "Are you trying to say I blew your mind?"

He smiled for real then and leaned down to my face. "You were the first I'd had in a long time. And you were amazing." Then he kissed my nose. "Thank you."

My arms slid up to his neck, and I pulled him down. "You haven't done anything to thank me for yet."

At that he closed the space between us, covering my mouth with his as he caught my ass and pulled me up against him. I held his neck, threading my fingers into his soft hair. Our mouths opened and our tongues collided, sending heat shooting straight between my legs.

His mouth broke away from mine briefly, "Where's the bedroom?" he asked.

Holding his neck, I looked over my left shoulder. "This way." I loosened my legs from his waist and he lowered me, following me to the small room in the back.

"I might need a bigger bed," I murmured as his hands moved from my waist under the front of my shirt to my breasts. I lay my head back against his shoulder, releasing a sigh as his fingers slid beneath my bra, caressing my nipples and filling my body with fire.

He kissed my neck, and I turned around slowly, finding his lips again as both our hands worked at our waists, unfastening buttons, lowering zippers. Two tugs and our shirts were off, and he reached out and grabbed me, lifting me up against his chest again. I reached back to remove my bra as my legs wrapped around his waist, my arms around his neck.

For a moment, we simply looked into each others' eyes. "You've had a pretty stressful night," he said. "I'll understand if you just want to sleep."

I slid my fingers through his hair, allowing myself to acknowledge for the first time since Princeton, how much I loved him.

"I want you to fuck my brains out," I smiled, leaning forward to nibble his lip.

He tilted his head up, quickly covering my mouth with his in a hungry kiss.

His lips moved to my jaw, tracing a burning line to my ear as he spoke. "I want to give you everything you want." Then he laid me back on the bed. I only had a second to wonder when he caught my thighs and pulled me to his mouth. His large hands squeezed my breasts, taunting my nipples as he bit at the front of my thong.

"Ooh, yes," I sighed, twisting with his touch. My eyes closed as my hips followed his movements, the tension in my pelvis growing with every expert touch. Finally, he slid his hands down my torso to my thong, which he removed. From there it was just his mouth kissing and pulling at my throbbing clit.

"Derek," I hissed as two thick fingers slipped inside me. Again, I let out a high-pitched whimper. He increased the pace, thrusting with his fingers as he pulled with his mouth, circling his tongue over my most sensitive parts. All at once the orgasm burst through me, and I cried out, pushing against his mouth and then pulling back.

"I want you inside me," I gasped, and he was up in an instant, dropping his shorts, revealing his massive cock. "Oh, please now." I gasped, but he froze, looking around my bedroom.

"Do you have a condom?" his voice was desperate.

"No," I gasped. His face fell, but I didn't care. I caught his hips and pulled him to me. "I know... but nothing's changed for me," I whispered. "There's been no one but you."

He caught my chin, looking into my eyes. "There's been no one but you," he confirmed, covering my mouth with his, stoking the heat raging in my stomach.

He pushed inside my slippery-wet entrance, both of us moaning in satisfaction. "Fuck, you feel so good," he growled against my neck, thrusting again deeper into me.

I nudged his shoulder, and he rolled onto his back, grasping my buttocks in both strong hands and lifting me up and down on top of him.

"I love that," I sighed against his neck, savoring the sensation of him, hot and full, hitting me in all the right places. "I've missed you so much," I gasped.

He groaned and lifted me faster, pounding me harder. I sat up and rocked my hips, rotating the angle so my clit got the full force of his thrusting. In seconds I was moaning and bucking. "Oh, god Derek, oh," I cried.

He rolled us over again so he was back on top, and I reached above my head, gripping the headboard. His mouth dropped to my breasts, and he gently kissed then bit my nipples, pulling another desperate cry from my throat as I shot over the edge, shuddering as I came. He kept pushing through my spasming muscles until in two sharp thrusts he slammed a hand against the wall behind my bed. "Fuck," he ground out as he went incredibly deep, coming hard and hot inside me.

He let out a few more ragged breaths, thrusting with each, and then he slowed, rolling us onto our sides, still buried between my legs. Little spasms continued pulsing through me, holding us together, and Derek hugged me tightly against his chest. My heart melted at the warmth of being surrounded in his arms, back in this wonderful place with him. With each gentle kiss to my forehead, my brow, my closed eyes, my love for him grew stronger.

We lay panting, holding each other for several long moments. It had been months since our last time, but nothing had changed. It was still as hot and breathtaking and beautiful as always. At last he slid out, holding me close in his arms and kissing my lips, gently parting them so our tongues could curl together. I smiled against his mouth, holding onto him, loving all of these pleasing sensations, basking in the afterglow of us together, reunited.

He rolled onto his back, pulling me against his chest and sliding his fingers down my back, tracing the lines in the way I loved.

"I missed you so much," I whispered. "It was terrible to be apart for so long."

He bent his elbow to place his hand under his head. "I felt the same way," he said with an exhale. "Every day, I would stare out the windows for the longest time wondering where you were, what you were doing. If you were happy, if you had made up with him. If you even thought about me."

My eyes grew damp, and I reached up to trace a finger down his perfect nose. "I did something very similar."

He lifted his chin to kiss my fingertip. "You did?"

I nodded. "Only I took it a step further. I would to go your company website and gaze at your picture. You're so handsome in that suit."

He smiled and changed our position, rolling us over and looking deep into my eyes. "I was afraid I'd become obsessed," he said softly. "Your blue eyes haunted me, and the way your voice cracks when you say my name when I'm inside you."

A wave of pleasure rushed through me at his words. He kissed the little hollow where my collarbones came together.

"I still have your necklace," he said, lifting his head to look at my face again. "I hope you'll take it back."

"Do you have it with you? I'll put it on right now."

"Yes, but stay here with me."

He moved to his side, and I snuggled close against his chest. His arms tightened around me as a deep sigh of satisfaction left his lips. Then he kissed the top of my shoulder.

"Melissa," he said, and the note of concern in his voice caused me to lean back and check his expression.

A line pierced my forehead. "What?"

He cleared his throat and looked down, then he pressed his lips against mine briefly. "I want to say this. It doesn't have to be tomorrow, but I need you to know—"

"What is it?" Concern tightened my chest. I had no idea what he needed me to know. I was afraid it might have something to do with the time we were apart. Maybe something he'd done?

He smiled at my expression. "I'm glad you look so worried, I guess."

I pushed back on his shoulder, sitting up in the bed. "If you don't finish that sentence…"

He rose to a sitting position beside me, catching my hand and pulling the back of it to his lips. "I want more than a week this time," he said, his voice turning gentle. "Much more." He paused and then held my gaze. "One day soon, when you're feeling whole again, I'm going to ask you to marry me."

My heart turned to liquid. "What?" My voice was a high whisper.

"I know," he quickly added. "You're just out of a bad marriage. You were married to a major league asshole. The ink isn't dry on your divorce papers. I'm not asking you for anything right now... But I will."

Tears clouded my vision. "And I'll say yes."

A smile broke across his face, brightening his beautiful blue eyes. He kissed me again, and I caught his cheeks, holding his lips against mine, opening my mouth and finding his tongue.

He kissed me again, longer, and I pushed him to his back, straddling him as I kissed his lips again and again. The heat was growing between my legs, and his palms scratched against the skin of my thighs, gently rising to my butt. My mouth broke from his and I let out a groan. "I want you again," I laughed, breathless.

He caught my hips and guided me down as he slid inside, filling me completely. We were off, and I couldn't stop smiling at the prospect of a lifetime together. Him with me, surrounding me, in me. Sharing everything.

And instead of pulling each other down, we'd be setting each other free.

"One request," I said, placing my palms flat on his chest.

"Oh, god, anything," he groaned, thrusting deeply.

His ravenous desire sent a wave of electricity through me. "I want to honeymoon in the desert."

"Done," he breathed, threading his fingers into my hair and pulling my mouth back to his.

I turned. "And at least once, we have to visit the family restroom together."

He growled a yes, making me laugh before he caught me in a deep, passionate kiss. My back arched and I moaned against his mouth. Wrapping my arms around his neck I rocked my hips, dreaming of that place of warm sunsets and gorgeous, fireside memories.

We'd toast to happy surprises, and we'd share many (after)glowing thank yous.

Epilogue:
Derek

Her dark hair fans out over the white pillow in perfect curls. Lifting one, I gently twist a shining spiral around my finger, sliding my thumb across the silky strand. The only thing more beautiful is her face, smooth and blissful in sleep.

I rest my head on my hand as I watch her breasts gently rise and fall, thinking of our last two months together. Early in December, I'd won her back by having that bastard Sloan arrested. I'd wanted to do more. Standing over his unconscious body in her living room, after he'd tried to hurt her again...

It had been years since I'd fought the urge to kill someone. If she hadn't been there, I might've.

Of course, he posted bail and was back hiding in his mansion a day later. He called in his team of lawyers, and Melissa backed down. I wasn't ready to let it go, but she begged me to drop it. She didn't want to be front-page news or dragged through a long ordeal. Reluctantly, I gave in to her. But every time I see that tiny silver scar near her hairline, it takes all my strength to keep from driving to Baltimore and beating him to a bloody pulp.

Only her bright eyes and happy smile calm those thoughts. And now she's having my baby. Our pre-Christmas slip up had been one too many, but I couldn't be happier. When Alison died, I thought my chances at being a father were over. That day, I'd walked away from everything having to do with love and family. I'd shut down, not even interested in trying again. Then six years later, my twisted mentor brought this gorgeous creature into my life.

The night I saw her in Scottsdale, I'd never seen such intense sadness in another person before. She was so beautiful, and yet she was visibly suffering. I knew how that felt. I'd struggled with intense sorrow, but somehow as the time had passed, my mourning period had ended, and I wanted her. I wanted to take all her unhappiness away with my love if she'd let me. And she did.

My hand moved from the curl around my finger to the top of her forehead, right where her dark hair met her ivory skin. Barely touching her, I remembered how incredible that first night had been — that whole week. It was a second chance. Until we'd had to part.

She stirs, dipping her chin the way she always does before opening her eyes. No use thinking about the days we were apart because now we're together, and I'm going to make her my wife.

Her gorgeous blue eyes blink open, and I can't help but smile. "Good morning."

"Were you watching me sleep?" Her soft voice is thick with sleep, and she turns her face into the pillow. Her slim bare shoulder lifts to her cheek, and just like that I have a hard-on. I want to pull her under me and kiss that shoulder, those lips, every part of her, but I control myself. She's just opened her eyes after all.

"You're beautiful when you sleep." I state the obvious, which always makes her blush. The fact this woman can't see how gorgeous she is drives me nuts. At the same time, it's part of the reason I love her so much. She's so focused on her work and her plans and us. She's completely unself-conscious.

"How are you feeling?" My hand travels down the length of her smooth back. Her body hasn't started showing she's pregnant yet. Well, her breasts are slightly larger, but they've always been the right size for me. Perfect handfuls.

She scoots into my chest, and immediately my arms go around her small frame. I love being able to lift her against me when we make love or surround her with protection. But, she's tough as nails. She lived through a year of hell and without anyone's help, she survived and made a new life for herself. That old urge to kill Sloan flickers again in my chest, but she banishes it by lifting her chin and kissing my throat.

"Hungry," she says, answering the question I'd left hanging. And with that she pushes above me, smiling. "I know I'm not really eating for two, but I swear, I don't remember ever craving breakfast like this. I want eggs with cheese and tomatoes and peppers..."

I laugh, lifting a clutch of dark curls off her shoulder and planting a kiss there. Her skin smells like roses and the ocean.

"And bacon!" she cries. "I want applewood-smoked bacon so bad right now. Doesn't that sound delicious?"

"You don't have to sell bacon to me." I pull her to me and kiss her nose.

Last night, her body had been wrapped around me in the most amazing way. As always, she'd cried out my name, shaking and moaning as she came hard and full over me. It was all I could do to hold out as she finished, she was so fucking gorgeous. I would do anything to keep this woman happy.

"I'm at a little disadvantage here," I say, sitting up with her in my arms. "You're a local now, but I'm still in Princeton. I don't know the best place to satisfy these new cravings."

Her arms go around my neck and she kisses my lips briefly. "Then let me show you!"

I smile, reaching for her, but she's gone — headed to the bathroom, leaving me to admire her perfect ass and tame this erection she's left me with. My sexual urges have to wait, it seems. Clearly, the mother of my child needs bacon.

"There's this historic little place in town," she calls from the hallway. I step into the boxer-briefs I tossed across the room last night after we returned home from dinner with Elaine and Patrick. Our clothes are a messy trail leading into the kitchen where we started.

Patrick relocated his base of operations to Wilmington last month. It was his early Christmas gift to Elaine, and it looked like he might beat me to the marriage punch. But I have a plan for today. And well, I already laid the ground work for it the night we made junior. Since then idea of us getting married has been theoretical, but today, I'd make it official.

"What's the name?" I call back, studying the picture of her and her mother in a weathered-wooden frame on her dresser. The two smile exactly alike, but her mother doesn't have Melissa's gorgeous blue eyes.

"The Sawmill. It's supposed to be really good," she says, returning to the room. I smile as she goes into her closet, completely unaware of how the sight of her naked, wearing only a thong and my floating-heart necklace affects me. "Did I say it's historic?"

She steps into a black skirt and I watch as she pulls a long-sleeved, faded red tee over her head. The vintage fabric hugs her braless torso in a way I want to. I can't help myself anymore. I go to her and pull her against my chest.

"I love you," I say, covering her mouth with mine. As always, she seems to melt.

She is such an amazing combination to me. This tiny firecracker, strong as a flint, able to survive the shit her asshole ex-husband had put her through. Yet when I kiss her, her entire body becomes fluid in my hands. It's very distracting.

I make sure she's standing before I completely release her to put on my shirt. Her nipples are erect as she grabs my fleece jacket off a chair and pulls it around her body. It's enormous on her, but she tucks her nose inside and inhales deeply.

"I'm keeping this when you go back," she says. "I might sleep in it."

Stepping into my jeans, her bedroom eyes have me fighting the return of that erection. "So you want to go to the Sawmill or not?"

"Yes," she laughs. "Bacon."

* * *

"There is no applewood-smoked bacon," I say as we study the menu.

The Sawmill restaurant is a traditional dive. Its exposed-wood interior is covered in tools of the logging trade, and the pages of our menus are covered in plastic. Still, I'm no snob. All the breakfast options look great to me, but I know how Mel's pregnancy has her craving specific things. I'd already been sent in search of Manhattan Key Lime pie the day after Christmas, and we have someone known as "Aunt Bea" on our speed-dial in case of emergencies.

She sighs. "It's okay. Regular bacon will do."

Our eyes meet, and the small, black-velvet box in my pocket feels hot as a coal waiting to be taken out and presented to her. I want to propose now, to claim her as mine, like nothing I'd ever wanted before, but I also want it to be special. So I wait.

"All bacon is wood-smoked, right?" I say as the waiter returns. "And Sawmill benedict? They've substituted gravy for hollandaise."

A little laugh escapes her throat. "Let's get that gravy on the side," she says. "And an omelet and a scrambler. And a juice and keep that coffee coming."

The waiter nods and leaves, and with a chuckle, I gesture for her to come around to my side of the table. As always, she's quick to comply. Sliding in next to me, she slips her arms around my neck and kisses my lips.

"I love you," she whispers. "Last night was..."

"Screaming Os, I'm the king and all that?"

I love the sound of her laughter. "I have never—"
Our eyes meet and her tone drops. She pretend-coughs, adjusting her story in an amusing fashion.

"You are *always* all of those things," she purrs.

My elbow is bent on the top of the bench behind her. I study her face a moment. "So this is where you want to stay. In this little town."

Our permanent residence is the one roadblock to our union we keep stumbling over.

"How can you even ask me that?" She turns, putting both elbows on the table as she lifts her coffee cup to her lips. "Living at the beach is a dream come true for most people."

"We don't have to sell your house," I repeat my argument, smiling at her cute stubbornness, as if adjusting her position can keep my words out. I move my hand to her waist and then under her shirt, spreading my palm over her bare stomach, thinking about what's growing there. "We can keep it, and you can come here as often as you like for vacations or whatever."

She lowers her cup and leans back, placing her hand on top of mine still covering her flat stomach. Our physical familiarity is another thing I love about her. She's unfazed by my hand against her skin. It's as if every one of my touches is not only welcome, but expected.

"We might as well quit now," she exhales. "If we can't even get through this impasse, I have no idea what makes us think we can handle more serious issues."

I can't help a laugh, and my hand goes from her stomach to her chin. I lift her delicate face and cover her small mouth with mine, tasting the bitter almost-chocolate flavor of the coffee as I part her lips, our tongues lightly touching. I want nothing more than to carry her back to that pretty, miniscule condo of hers and fuck her twenty ways from Sunday. Show her just how strong our love is.

Releasing her face, I look into her now-darkened eyes. "Choosing a home base is actually a pretty big decision," I say. "I think if we can decide on a place where we'll both be happy, it's proof we can handle anything."

She's ready to relent. I know by her expression my kiss has left her willing to do anything I ask. God, I love her so much.

"Derek." When she says my name that way, I can't tell if she's aware I'll do anything she asks. "Sloan asked me to leave here. And it was the most unhappy decision I've ever made in my life. I never want to make that mistake again."

Her words sting, but I understand her fears. I saw what she survived. My fingers trace a light path down her cheek as I exhale. "For one, I'm not Sloan," I say, keeping my voice gentle. "And for two, we don't have to make this decision today."

She blinks and her smile returns. The waiter also returns with our orders, and I kiss the side of her head. As he puts three orders of eggs—poached, scrambled, and wrapped in an omelet—in front of us, all served with sides of sausage, bacon, and ham. We spread out the plates and get ready to sample, share, and devour.

"Delicious," she smiles, lifting a thin slice of salty pork and taking a big bite.

* * *

After breakfast we head down to the shore in front of Melissa's place. My office is still closed for the New Year's holiday, which I spent wrapped in my lady's arms, but I'll be heading back to Princeton in another day.

She inhales deeply as we walk, and the strong breeze pushes her dark hair off her shoulders. It also whips her black skirt around her still-slim hips, and she has my fleece jacket zipped all the way up. It's like a dress on her.

"I have an idea," she says, slanting those baby blues at me, "What if you stay in Princeton and I stay here, and we just met up for conjugal visits?"

I decide to take her challenge and raise it. "That sounds like a reasonable plan. I can probably go a month between visits. How about you?"

Her expression almost costs me my poker face. Clearly she did not expect me to concede to her ridiculous offer, and it appears she might cry. Her brow melts into a frown, which she tries to lift and fails.

"I was only teasing," she says in a voice that twists my insides. "I can barely stand us being apart for a week."

It's impossible to hold out after that, and I scoop her small frame against my chest. "And I can barely stand two hours." I lean forward and kiss her again, and as always, her body melts into mine. It awakens my urge to take her.

"I've been thinking about you all morning," I say. "Let's go back to bed."

Her nose wrinkles as she laughs. "Maybe it is better for us to be separated for now. We're way too horny to get anything done in the same city."

Her use of the pronoun *we* is all I need. My eyes meet hers, and I see that fire brewing in them. It's only grown stronger since she's been pregnant, and I know from our first encounters she doesn't shrink from being risqué.

Glancing over my shoulder, I verify that we're alone. No one is out on this cold, January day but us, and we have the beach to ourselves. Still, I use discretion, leading her away from the open shoreline into a nearby patch of beach scrub. It's not only private, it's out of the breeze and less chilly.

I sit on the soft sand, pulling her onto my lap. Skirts and thong underwear might be my favorite clothing combination. My hands are up her thighs and caressing her clit as fast as our lips can find each other's. Her arms are tight around my neck and her whimpers slip out between passes of my mouth over hers. My erection is straining against the zipper of my jeans, and I want nothing more than to be buried in her tight, wet opening this instant. I've wanted it all morning.

Her hand goes to my waist to unfasten my pants, and when her slim fingers wrap around me, the memory of her mouth closing over my tip almost sends me off. The first time she gave me head, I almost shot down her throat it was so good. But I fight to distract myself from those thoughts and get her off instead. I've been on edge all morning, and her hand sliding up and down my dick isn't helping. My fingers press into her wet opening as my thumb caresses her clit. I can tell by her breathing, she isn't far behind me.

"Ooh," she moans, sending shockwaves through my shaft. I want to be inside her so badly. Quickly, I slide down the zipper on my jacket and lift her shirt, catching one of her taut nipples in my mouth. Her breasts are gorgeous right now. I give one a little suck, and she sighs with pleasure. I almost lose control.

"I need to be inside you," I whisper, moving my mouth to her ear. I give her lobe a little bite, and she shivers. At once, she shifts her position, moving her thong aside and dropping down on my cock.

"Uuh," I can't help but groan as her warm passage envelops me. I wanted to lay her back and pound her hard on the sand, but I'm not sure she's finished yet. Gripping her ass, I lifted her up and down, keeping my thumb on her clit, massaging her.

Her arms tighten around my neck as her breasts rise under my chin with every lift. It's fucking amazing and almost more than I can take. "Derek," she gasps in my ear, and I know we're hitting the right spot. She's lifting herself on me now without my even helping her.

"Don't stop," she gasps, but I'm barely touching her as she works me. I'm doing everything in my power to hold out while she finishes. Her inner muscles tighten on me as her orgasm begins, pulling and releasing. It's far better than hands or a mouth, feeling her come around my cock.

"Oh, shit," I groan, but I can't stop it. Her inner workings have me shooting off inside her, and the pleasure momentarily blacks out my thoughts. All I know is me buried deep in her gorgeous body, my orgasm primed and extended by hers. Instinctively, my grip on her ass tightens, and I'm lifting her harder and faster up and down as I finish.

A hoarse moan scrapes from her throat, and as I continue moving her, more noises follow. Her thighs quiver, her knees press into the sand, and she's riding me now. She's making it, and after several more movements, she drops, arms draped around my neck, head on my shoulder, aftershocks slowly subsiding.

"God, I love you," I murmur, kissing her neck, traveling with my lips behind her ear, causing her to shiver again and laugh.

She sits up and holds my face, her cheeks pretty and pink from her climax. "I love you," she says in a breathy voice.

Our warmth is like our own little world. Sure, we might violate a public decency law every so often, but we take care to keep it secret and unseen. Without moving her away, staying buried deep between her thighs, I reach for my pants pocket.

"I've been trying to find the right time to give you this," I say, fumbling for the black velvet box. Her eyes widen, and instantly she's off my lap, pulling down her skirt and sitting beside me on the sand. She takes the small box, but doesn't open it.

Pulling my jeans up, I catch her eyes on mine, and I can see her enthusiasm. "Is this what I think it is?" Her voice is still breathless.

A smile crosses my lips. "I can't read your mind."

For a moment, she only holds it, and my stomach tightens in anticipation. I took a chance on this ring—it isn't the traditional diamond, but I figured since we've both been married once before, we might be up for something different.

With a quick glance back at me, she pulls the top open and then gasps. Inside is a square-cut blue sapphire ring encased in platinum with tiny white diamonds all around it. It's an art deco style, and it matches her eyes and the sea perfectly.

I take the box back and lift the ring out. Her fingers tremble slightly as I hold her hand in both of mine.

"Melissa Jones," I say, keeping the ring poised and ready. "Will you marry me?"

My eyes travel from her hand to the heart floating at her neck to her eyes, which are now shining. All I can remember is that night in the desert when she'd wanted to say she loved me. I'd gone immediately to the nearest jewelry store still open and bought the first thing they had with a heart on it. She'd stolen mine then, and I knew the only way to get it back would be to marry her.

With a hiccupped breath, her face breaks into a smile. "Yes," she nods. "I already told you I'd say yes, but yes, yes, yes." She laughs, wrapping her arms around my neck. Our mouths meet and my hand fumbles back down only briefly pausing before sliding around her waist, drawing her close against me. I love how our bodies move together so easily. We belong to each other.

"If you want me to move to Princeton, I will," she says, kissing my lips once more before resting her forehead against my cheek. I know right then she's saying she'll do whatever I want, and that's the funny thing with power. When the one you love gives it to you, you start looking for every opportunity to give it back or at the very least, use it for her happiness.

"I don't want you to leave the place you love," I say, my hands moving under her shirt to her breasts. I lay her back on the sand and push up her tee. Her belly isn't the slightest bit round yet, but we've both heard the little heart in there beating so fast.

I kiss her right below the navel. "It's not a bad drive. Let's get this little person here and then we'll decide what to do."

Her slim fingers thread into my hair as she exhales deeply. My wife. My beautiful wife who's given me another chance at a family. Even though my instinct resists, and my inner drive is to be the boss, she has my heart. I'll do anything for her.

I hold her close, resting my cheek on her skin, loving her. She continues lacing her fingers through my hair, and we listen to the soft noise of the breakers. It's as if we're on our own private island together. After a while, we slowly stand, repositioning our clothes. Our fingers entwine as we walk back to her condo.

"I was thinking if it's a girl, we can call her Edith. If it's a boy, Dexter."

"No and maybe." I say curtly.

As tiny as she is, Mel is unexpectedly strong. She jerks my arm hard, and I can't suppress a laugh. "Edith is a terrible name for a baby."

"It's a family name," she cries.

"And I don't know about Dexter."

"I think it's cute. We can call him Dex."

"I was thinking Scott or Cactus Flower—for where we met."

Her brow wrinkles. "You cannot be serious."

I laugh again. So perhaps we have the housing situation on hold—now begins a new round of debate. Baby names. Knowing how stubborn we both are, I figure we can prolong this argument into the child's fifth birthday when it can decide.

She's still fussing, and I know the one way to win any argument with Melissa. But I'll save my next win for the bedroom.

~ The End. ~

If you enjoyed this book by this author, please consider leaving a review at Amazon, Barnes & Noble, or **Goodreads**!

* * *

Want a different view of the story? Put the companion novel, *One to Keep* on your TBR list today!

One to Keep
by Tia Louise

WARNING: Mature themes, strong language and sexual content. Recommended for adult readers (18+) only!

There's a new guy in town...

"Patrick Knight. Single, retired Guard-turned private investigator. I was a closer. A deal maker. I looked clients in the eye and told them I'd get their shit done. And I did..."

Patrick doesn't do "nice."
At least, not anymore.

After his fiancé cheats, he follows up with a one-night stand and a disastrous office hook-up. His business partner (Derek Alexander) sends him to the desert to get his head straight--and clean up the mess.

While there, Patrick meets Elaine, and blistering sparks fly, but she's not looking for any guy. Or a long-distance relationship.

Patrick's ready to do anything to keep her, but just when it seems he's changed her mind, the skeletons from his past life start coming back.

Standalone, M/F, HEA

Available January 16, 2014; **Add it on Goodreads today!**

Acknowledgments

Writing a novel has always been a dream of mine. Telling stories that sweep readers into a lovely dream or a fantasy of happiness is a gift, and I hope I've done it well.

Special thanks to Hart Johnson, Kate Roth, and Magan Vernon, the best critique partners a gal could have. Thanks to Regina Wamba for the gorgeous cover design. Thanks to Giselle and KP for exceptional marketing.

Thanks to the readers, reviewers, and book bloggers, who took a chance on an unknown author. In particular, thanks to Karrie, Lisa, Nevena, Linda, JAnne, Chantelle, Jennifer, Patrycja, Nikki, and Brianne. You ladies encouraged me more than you can possibly know.

Thanks also to the writers I can't name here who have provided invaluable support and encouragement.

Finally, thanks to the love of my life and to my family for sharing me as I wrote. You've given me the gift of pursuing my dream.

Thank you. <3

ABOUT THE AUTHOR

Tia Louise is a former journalist, world-traveler, and collector of beautiful men (who inspire <u>all</u> of her stories... *wink*) — turned wife, mommy, and novelist.

It's possible she has a slight truffle addiction. And she will never look at a family restroom the same way again.

One to Hold is her debut adult romance.

One to Keep releases January 16, 2014; Add it on Goodreads today!

* * *

Connect with Louise!
On Facebook:
https://www.facebook.com/AuthorTiaLouise
On Twitter: https://twitter.com/AuthorTLouise
On Pinterest: http://pinterest.com/AuthorTiaLouise
On Instagram: www.instagram.com/AuthorTLouise
Email: allnightreads@gmail.com

Made in the USA
Lexington, KY
07 January 2016